A SUMMER'S EXILE

Andre Gould

A Summer's Exile

THE GAY MEN'S PRESS
LONDON

To Stuart and Julie, without whom...
&
L W, for taking an interest in all those commas.

First published 1996 by GMP Publishers Ltd,
P O Box 247, London N6 4BW, England

World copyright © 1996 Andre Gould

British Library Cataloguing in Publication Data
Gould, Andre
A Summer's Exile
1.Young adult fiction, English
I.Title
823.9'14[J]
ISBN 0 85449 202 X

Distributed in North America by
Inbook, Login Publishers Consortium,
1436 West Randolph Street, Chicago, IL 60607

Distributed in Australia by Bulldog Books,
P O Box 155, Broadway, NSW 2007

Printed and bound in the EU by Nørhaven A/S, Viborg, Denmark

Contents

1

Meeting

I was standing on the riverbank, my feet in the water, skipping stones. I hoped at least one would reach the other side, but I knew they wouldn't. My river was much too wide for that.

The river ran past our fields, but no one ever came to this spot. Pa sometimes went upstream to check the pump. Ma never came here at all. I'd decided to spend that hot sunny morning skipping stones. I looked around and filled my pockets with the best ones I could find. Once I'd been the best. Now it didn't matter any more, but I was bored and had nothing else to do.

After I had warmed up and gotten back into it, I lost all sense of time. All I heard was the skip, skip, plop! of each stone that my hand sent bouncing across the smooth surface of my quiet river.

Which was why I didn't hear the kid slide down the bank and walk up behind me.

"Hi there!"

I nearly jumped out of my skin. If it hadn't been for a bit of quick footwork, I would have fallen right into the river. The stone in my right hand flew high in the air above me and splashed into the river about ten yards from where I stood. It was a good flat one that I just knew would have been my best.

"Darn!" I didn't know which made me more mad, losing the stone or hearing someone else on my riverbank. Mad as hell, I turned to see a kid about the same age as me standing a few feet away. All I saw was a pair of new blue jeans, a T-shirt and a baseball cap, with long fair hair poking out underneath. It looked like a girl in boy's clothes.

The kid lifted his head a little. I was wrong. It was a boy I'd never seen before.

"Sorry," he said, seeing how he'd startled me.

"Wh.. wh.. what did you want to go and do th.. that for?" I asked.

"You didn't hear me from up there," he said, pointing up the bank to where the dusty grass grew. "So I came down. I didn't mean to scare you."

"W.. w.. well, you did." I wanted to hit him for scaring me half to death and for interrupting my stone-skipping session. And just for being there, on my riverbank.

"What're you doing?" he asked, before I could ask him the same question. He was sure testing my patience. This was my place. I was the one to ask questions.

"Nuh.. Nuh.. nothin'," I said.

"You were skipping stones."

I kept my mouth shut.

"Can I watch?" he asked.

I didn't want him to. I didn't know what he was doing here. He could've been sent to spy on me. But maybe he was okay. I could always get rid of him later. I could make just about any kid run away.

"Sh.. sh.. sure," I said, taking out a stone and leaning back to throw it, hoping it wouldn't end up like the last one. It was a good one. It skimmed across the water four times and fell slowly into the middle of the river.

Maybe the kid was an admirer, I thought as I brought out another stone. He'd been secretly watching me from the top of the riverbank and finally got up the courage to come down and meet his hero. Me – some hero.

The next stone was as good as the last. I knew I was good. Maybe the kid wanted my autograph, like I'd seen people ask that Marilyn Monroe on television. I'd have to think about it; I hadn't written my name in a long time. Anyway, I wasn't going to stop skippin' stones just for him. He'd just have to wait. Besides, I bet he didn't have a bit of paper. I could have signed his arm, I supposed. But I bet he didn't have a pen either.

The next stone plopped down in the middle of the river, gracefully, the way a good stone should. Even as I threw it, getting the right angle, I knew the kid wasn't going to keep silent for ever but was going to ask me something else. I was right, he did.

"Can I try?" he asked.

Now let's get one thing straight, I thought, before I turned back to face him. This is my riverbank. Private and out of the way of everyone and their opinions about me. It's the only place I can go where no one's going to bother me. No one, especially not a strange kid with girl's hair in a baseball cap and new jeans!

Besides, watching your hero skip stones is one thing. You always want to watch someone who's better than you. Giving it a try's different! You just keep your mouth shut and we'll get on fine, I thought. In fact, maybe you should just go and...

Before I could get a word out, he pulled the cap off his head. My mouth hung open. He was the most beautiful kid I'd seen in all my twelve short, ugly years. His hair was the lightest and finest of browns. It was so light it was almost blond. It hung over his pale face like the frame of a picture. It started as a long fringe over his forehead and fell over his cheeks, hiding his ears like fancy theatre curtains. His eyebrows were the same color. I could hardly see them under the fringe.

In the middle were the brightest green eyes I had ever seen. They were like living, colored jewels sparkling in the sunlight. As I stared into them, they vanished behind the thickest pair of eyelashes I had ever seen on a boy. Then his eyes reappeared, even brighter than before.

His nose was small and straight. His thin red lips hung over his neat, perfectly shaped chin. His skin reminded me of my baby cousin's, smooth as the white cream that my Ma dabbed on her face every night.

Whoever had cut his hair knew the effect it would have on the people he met. His whole face begged to be admired, even more than my skipping stones. If I'd seen him in town, I'd have swore he was a Momma's boy. Which is probably why he wore the baseball cap, to hide his hair and face from the people would just stare at him. Like me.

He was nothing like me. My hair was a black, curly mess. My Pa made me have it cut real short back and sides which made the hair on the top of my head stick up like a heap of dirty cotton. I reckoned I should have it cut the way I wanted but there was no way I could tell Pa that. A couple of times I'd thought of cutting it all off with the kitchen scissors just to spite him, but I didn't dare. Just once a month I did as I was told and walked straight to the barber and came straight back home. The men waiting next to me could order what they wanted — "just trim the back" or "a quarter of an inch off the sides" — and the barber obliged, but I had to get skinned and walk back home with a prickly draft on my neck.

So there I stood with my hair a mess, wearing nothing but a pair of overalls that had holes just about everywhere, while this kid in front of me had everything I didn't. The way he stood there, just waiting, watching me, showed he didn't have a care in the world. It was obvious he didn't know who I was, or the chance he was taking standing like he did on my riverbank. *I might still chase him away,* I thought.

But I didn't. Seeing him standing there well within my reach, all innocent and delicate, did something to my insides. I didn't know what it was, but it kind of hurt and it kind of made me feel good and it just sat there.

I must have been staring at the kid for too long, cause he asked again, "Can I try. Please?"

I don't know what he was thinking about me standing there all silent like that. I wasn't about to tell him what effect his looks had on me. Nor what I felt. Jealous and angry. I wanted to kill him. I hated the way he looked. I hated the fact any kid could look like him and not be plain ugly, like me.

It wasn't natural. But I couldn't think how it could be anything else. It was like old Ma Nature had gone soft in her choice of looks for this kid. He looked like an angel and that made me want to throw up. I could see him singing hymns in the choir and getting gushy looks from all the grownups.

He had it made. All the women in town would swoon as they fought to pat his long hair and admire him. Yeucch!

"Sh.. sure," I said, picking out the smallest stone in my pocket. I wasn't about to let him have my best one, the one I'd hidden inside the front pocket. He'd only waste it. I didn't even know why I was letting him have the small stone, the way I hated his looks, but anyhow I did.

He took it and placed it carefully in the palm of his small, delicate hand the same way I did when I threw. I watched him taking his time, his long fair hair dropping back off his face as he leant to one side and back a little, just as I did when preparing to skip my stones. Then, with more strength than I thought possible a kid like him would have, he whipped his arm quickly forward and let fly.

His hair swished forward, covering his entire face as the stone shot out of his hand. He shook the strands away and watched the stone sail through the air and bounce on and off the surface of the water four times before it dropped into the depths, its energy spent.

He sure knew how to skip.

"Great sh.. shot!" leapt from my mouth before I could stop it.

Darn! I thought. The kid was good. I'd given him my worst stone and he'd made it look so easy. It was almost as if he was better than any of us Summer Skippers, better even than me.

We had gotten together last summer, before everything went wrong. About five or six got together most days to mess around and skip stones until darkness sent us home. We'd had a really great time.

"Thanks. Got any more?" he asked, holding out his right hand.

What did he want me to do? Give him another stone from my pocket until they all disappeared? I'd spent ages looking for them; I wasn't going to give them away, now that I'd seen how good he was. I wasn't going to give him the chance to beat the ex-champ of the Summer Skippers, even if he didn't know who I was.

Or maybe he did and he was just testing me.

"S.. sorry," I said, holding out my hands to show him they were empty. "W.. we could look for m.. more," I suddenly said, surprising myself.

He shook his head. "It's okay. Anyway, I got to be going," he said.

Thought so, I told myself, he's chicken! He's afraid to get dirty looking for them in the mud.

"Wh.. where d'you come from?" I asked, cause I didn't want him to go, not yet anyway. I wanted to know who he was and if we'd meet again. I kind of liked him being here, even if it was my river. And I wanted to know if he was new in town and if the others in the gang would find out about him beating the champ with a stupid little stone that was no good to anyone.

Then I remembered. I wasn't in the gang anymore. I would never be one of the Summer Skippers again.

"My Pa bought the old place up by the road," the kid said. "We moved in yesterday."

"Th.. the old Parker place?"

"Yeah. You know it?"

"Sh.. sure. It's right n.. next to our place." Of course I knew the Parker place. I always hid in the old barn when I needed to get away from it all. Then I thought if this kid and his family had moved in, I couldn't do that any more. But it didn't seem to matter. Something inside my head was cheering and clapping just like those highschool girls did for the football team, waving their pom-poms all over the field.

"See you tomorrow then?" he asked, as he started climbing back up the bank.

"Expect s.. so," I said, shrugging my shoulders, not committing myself too much, publicly anyway. "After breakfast, m.. maybe."

"Okay, bye." He gave a kind of wave as he reached the top, then turned to run quickly up the path I had made by walking across the bottom two fields of my father's farm every day. He reached the dirt track that one way led to our place and the other way back to the road and the old Parker place. Even after I couldn't see him any more, I could see the dust his legs kicked up from the sun-baked earth.

The kid must have seen me yesterday from his old man's pick-up. Maybe I was walking down to the river and that's how he knew where to find me. Or maybe he was just exploring. Anyhow, it looked as if he wanted to be friends. I thought I did too, but I didn't know how long it would last. Sooner or later his Pa or mine would find out and that would be the end of it.

I took out the last of the stones from my pockets and set about practising my skills for tomorrow. I was determined to wipe the floor with the kid. There was no way he was going to beat the champ of the Summer Skippers. But I didn't want to beat him too hard. I might hurt his feelings.

That was a strange thought and it made me jerk my arm. I watched as the stone skipped once, twice and then dive into the river, wasted. Darn! It was a good thing the kid was no longer around to see. I was suddenly not so sure I'd beat him as I had been. That had been a good stone too, nice and flat, big and guaranteed to skip at least five times.

What was wrong with me?

It wasn't lack of skill that made me blow it. I just wasn't doing it right. Somehow I didn't want to do it alone any more. I wanted to do something different and didn't know what. But I didn't want to stay by the river any more.

I scrambled up the bank and headed for home, skipping and running on the way. Soon as I caught myself acting like that, I stopped and started walking the way I always did, kind of slow and kicking up dust with the toes of my old boots. I didn't want Ma or Pa asking what had gotten into me. The kid was my secret and I was going to keep it that way as long as I could.

2

Competing

He turned up right on time, just as the sun was starting to heat another day of the long, hot summer. My river was as calm that morning as it was every morning. For a time I watched the water glide by, not wanting to disturb it with even one stone. Then I started to throw a few, just to prove to myself I could still do it. I might go for a swim later, I thought, after I'd shown the kid who was the champ.

"Hi," he shouted. I turned and saw him slide down the dusty riverbank on his butt. It looked like he didn't care what happened to his jeans and boots, even though they were a lot newer than the clothes I was wearing. I had the same overalls on as yesterday and a red check shirt. It wasn't as scruffy as the ones I usually wore. He had a clean white shirt with two breast pockets. It looked neat. He wasn't wearing his cap and his hair was all over the place, but he didn't look so much like a girl as the first time I'd seen him.

"Been here long?" he asked, as if he was figuring out how much practise I'd had already.

"N.. nah." I wasn't going to let him think I was scared of losing.

I watched him pick a few stones and skip them. He threw really hard for a kid his size. His arm sort of whipped out like he was punching someone in the gut. Even with small stones he got a good three or four. Then he found a big flat one and threw an easy five. Each skip seemed to last as long as the one before and the stone was more than halfway across the water before it sank.

I had to beat it. I was lucky and got a six. It didn't reach as far as his five, but it was good enough. He looked at me. I looked at him. Without saying anything, we'd begun.

There was a part of the river where the water was so calm it looked like it never moved. I picked another good flat stone and made six and a half there. It made me feel good. It wasn't a pitch and skip, but an even skip, skip, plop! that hardly made a noise as it bounced across the water.

His next one was a four, then four and a half, while I did a three then a four. I didn't know why, but half the time I was throwing good and half the time I was making a mess of it. I kept watching him to see how he was doing and that kind of threw me off balance.

I kept seeing his long, shiny hair swishing about his pale face and I kept wanting to sweep it back so he could see proper. And there was something funny about the way he looked, all determined, but not with his face screwed up like lots of kids. One minute I'd think he looked kind of beautiful and the next minute I'd turn away in disgust, cause he just looked too beautiful. I kept hearing that word in my head, beautiful, beautiful, and I didn't like it. It didn't sound right at all.

I don't know how long we kept skipping, matching shot for shot. I think he got tired sooner than me, cause I started winning more. Then he got better again and it was tough keeping ahead of him.

We'd already finished one pile of stones and had almost finished the second. I didn't want to be the first one to stop and so I kept going, even though my arm and shoulder were starting to hurt.

"Want to stop?" he asked.

"Okay, if you're t.. tired." I shrugged, glad he'd asked to stop first. I reckoned I'd won the contest, but I didn't want to say so, in case it made him feel bad. "J.. just one more shot."

Together we threw our last stones across the water. Mine got four and a half. His only made four. We stood there for a moment, neither of us saying anything.

"Want to fish?" the kid suddenly asked, like he was challenging me to some other sport. He had a funny kind of look on his face, like he was sure he'd catch a bigger fish than me. He should've known I fished a lot too. I didn't have much else to do all day.

"G.. got no poles," I said.

"I got mine. It's up there." He pointed back up at the path. "Where's yours?"

"Home," I said.

"We can go get it."

I didn't want to, but I couldn't tell him that.

"That's your place, isn't it?" he asked, pointing at my Pa's house.

I nodded.

"Let's go." He started climbing the bank. There was nothing I could do but follow.

"What's your name?" he asked suddenly when we got to the top.

"M.. Mickey."

"I'm Steppin," he said boldly, nodding his head a little as he emphasized the word. His hair fell over his face again. He brushed it back with his hand, tucking bits of it behind his ears.

"S.. S.. Stephan?" I tried to repeat.

"No," he looked almost mad. "Steppin. I chose it. I like it. It's what I call myself. It's what other people call me."

I wanted to ask how come he chose that name but I didn't dare. Sometimes I couldn't open my mouth without everyone getting mad at me. Anyhow, his name was fine by me. "S.. Steppin," I said carefully. "It's a good name."

"Thanks," he said. "Let's go."

I'd almost forgotten, but I couldn't stop him. He picked up his pole and off we went. His rod was like mine, the cheapest you could buy, not much more than a piece of wood with cotton line, a hook and a wooden float. Still, if you were real quiet and real careful and slow you could catch a lot of fish with a pole like that.

As we walked up to my place, I looked around to see if I could see Pa anywhere, but I couldn't. There was no one in sight, just my home nearby and Steppins further off. It was on the same kind of land as ours, but not on the river. That was why no one had bought it, Pa said; it had no irrigation. I wondered if Steppin's Pa knew that before he bought the place, and in the middle of a drought too. My Pa was finding it difficult enough keeping our place going with the pump. I didn't think the Parker place even had a well.

We were halfway to my place, when I realized why he called himself by that name — Steppin. I was going kind of slow, wondering what I could say to make him change his mind, and I noticed the way he walked. It was a kind of bounce, light, the way the stones sometimes skipped across the water. It wasn't the way most boys walked, but it was nothing like a girl's walk either, the way they sway from side to side, their butts rolling around all stupid.

The way Steppin walked was like he didn't place his full weight on the ground. I looked at it and tried to copy it but couldn't. Then I thought I was wrong to try. It was his walk. If he saw me copying him, he'd think I was laughing at him. And I wasn't. No way. I'd never laugh at Steppin the way other kids laughed at me.

When I stopped trying and looked up again, I saw we'd almost reached the kitchen. And Steppin was about to walk in as if was his house and I was the stranger come to visit.

"Hold on!" I said. "If my P.. Pa's in there, you'll have to hide."

He looked at me kind of weird but didn't say anything. With my finger to my mouth, I made him stand on one side of the kitchen door so that if Pa was in the kitchen, he wouldn't see Steppin when I walked in.

"Wait here," I whispered, pointing my finger at his boots, like a grownup speaking to a five-year-old.

"How come?" he asked.

"Because I say so!" My voice was sharp but still low. I couldn't tell him how come. There was just too much to tell. Besides, what would he think of me if he knew it all?

"I'll be quick," I said. Hoping he wouldn't move, I opened the screen door and rushed through the kitchen. There was no one there.

"That you, Mickey?" Ma shouted from the parlor.

"Yeah, Ma."

"What're you doin'?"

"N.. nothin'. Goin' f.. fishin'." I raced up the stairs before she could say anything, making loads of noise, which she wouldn't like, but I had to get my fishing pole and hooks before Steppin disobeyed me.

I looked all over my room but couldn't find a new hook for the line. Then I remembered the box where I kept my secret things. It was in my bottom dresser drawer, under piles of clothes I used to wear to that place. The hooks there weren't as rusty as the one on the end of my pole. Though I fished a lot, I'd hardly caught anything lately. It must have been the rusty hook that kept the fish away. Either that or I didn't try hard enough.

I jumped down the stairs, fishing pole in hand, and dashed back into the kitchen. I could have died right there. Steppin was sitting at our breakfast table, swinging his legs to and fro, obviously unhappy that he'd had to wait for me.

Ma was still in the parlor, probably doing housework of some kind or other. She worked hard every day to keep our house tidy and got no thanks from me or Pa.

"Wh.. what are you doing?" I hissed to Steppin, pulling on his arm to try and get him off the chair. "Do you want to get me a s.. skinnin'?"

"Mickey?" I heard Ma call from the front room.

Steppin still hadn't moved. At least he was keeping his mouth shut. Then he saw how I scared I was by what Ma might say if she came in and saw him. He let me pull him off the chair and push him towards the door.

"Yeah, Ma?" I shouted as I eased Steppin out, trying to avoid the squeak of the screen door.

"Hide! Quick!" I hissed at him, as he stood not moving on the outside step. "There," I said, pointing to the empty water barrel by the side of the house.

"You always leave your guests outside our door?" Ma's voice was nearer.

"N.. no, Ma," I said as I came back in. What was she thinking of? I never had any guests.

"Well, let me see him." Ma came into the kitchen, stood there with a rag in her hand. She didn't look mad, the way she sometimes does.

"What about Pa? He won't like it, Ma." Besides, I didn't want Steppin to come in. I didn't want him to meet Ma or Pa.

"He's in the top field. I packed him lunch. He'll be there all day if the tractor holds out. Who's your friend?"

I turned and saw Steppin standing there, watching the two of us like we were some kind of rodeo. I knew then that Steppin didn't obey any rules when it came to doing what he was told. That way he was pretty much just like me.

"This is Steppin, Ma."

"How d'you do?" said Steppin.

"Steppin," said Ma, like it was a regular name. "You and your folks just moved in by the road, right?"

"Yes, ma'am."

"You goin' fishing?" Ma asked me.

"Yeah, Ma," I said, still kind of shook up and relieved she wasn't going to tell Pa about Steppin.

"You be careful down by that river. Your father's pump's going. Don't touch it, else he'll tan your hide, you hear?"

"Yeah, Ma" ... "Let's go," I said to Steppin.

"Goodbye, ma'am," Steppin said as I kind of pushed him off the step.

"Mickey!" Ma called as I grabbed Steppin by his wrist and started dragging him across the yard.

"See you later, Ma," I shouted as we ran toward the door in the back of the barn. I was afraid she was changing her mind and was going to tell Pa. Maybe she just wanted to go on at me about tidying my room or make me brush what was left of my hair. Or the hundred other things she was always going on about. Or the end of the summer holidays and what would happen then.

I heard the screen door open as we made the shelter of the barn.

"Mickey!"

"We gotta go," I said. "If she finds me, she'll s.. start talkin' about... that place again." I pulled him right through the open doors and round the side of the barn, out of sight of the house. We couldn't run any further or she'd see us, so I pushed Steppin down and we sat against the wall. He looked at me but didn't say anything.

"Mickey, you get back here when I'm talking to you!" Ma shouted. We didn't move. She knew where I was. If she wanted, she could come and get me.

We waited. I knew Ma would either turn the corner to where we hid, hunched against the barn, or we'd hear the screen door slam. The door slamming would mean she'd given up. But I wasn't sure if she was really mad. Sometimes her temper was so bad, I'd stay late at the river or doze in the fields, until she cooled down. But today she'd been okay.

The door slammed. "It's clear," I said. I knew the screen would be swinging on its squeaky hinges for ages, back and forth, juddering from the impact. We stood up and walked away from the barn, hidden from Ma's view from the kitchen, fishing poles over our shoulders, like two soldiers going off to war.

Fishing

Down by the river I found the old trowel I used to dig bait and the rusty can I kept the bait in. We stuck our poles in the ground and got to digging in the mud for worms. All the while I never looked at him, but I could see him, like I was staring at him all the time.

There was his long fair hair shadowing his emerald eyes, the kind of hair that all the women in town just loved to tussle. Then there were his thin red lips, like a cherub's. And that angelic look, like he wasn't quite real. Women would want to lift his chin with their fingers, just to look at him full in the face. He was everything every mother wished for in a son. Ma had felt the same way, I could tell.

I wanted to go "Yeuch!" It made me want to wrap myself up and throw me away in a trash can. No one would ever want me in the way Steppin was wanted.

I found a worm and stuck it on my hook. I was thinking how I hated all grownups, how jealous I was of Steppin. I wanted to scream at the unfairness of it all.

"I got a juicy one," Steppin said. "Should catch a whopper." I looked up as he showed me his worm on the hook. And all at once I stopped feeling mad, because he was here with me and we had all day together.

"Sh.. sure will," I said, and showed him mine.

I showed him the best place to fish, beside a row of tangled bushes overhanging the river, where the fish hid away from the strong sun. The water was calm there, hardly moving at all.

I threw my line out over the river. The hook dipped and the worm disappeared. I could feel the pole shake a little, as the worm continued to struggle.

Steppin threw his line a little upstream from me like he'd been fishing all his life. He didn't have a proper fishing rod with a reel, just a line on the end of a pole, with a hook and crude wooden float. The same as mine. I watched him a little, then felt a tug on my line and the pole bend, almost pulling free from my hand. I gripped it tighter and held on.

It was a big fish that thrashed about in the water, two pounds if it was an ounce. I hauled it towards the shallows, afraid it was going to break free. "Get it, quick," I cried as it leapt out of the water, trying to thrash itself off my new hook.

Steppin stuck his pole firmly in the ground and rushed over to where my fish was throwing itself about, kicking off his shoes and rolling up his jeans before he waded into the river. His legs were pale and thin, I noticed.

"Here, boy, come on, come on home to Papa," I heard him call as he chased the fish in the shallows, trying to hook his finger under its gills. Then he changed his tack, lunged for the fish and grabbed the middle of its back, fixing it firmly to the river bed as its head and tail continued to thrash.

"Quick, pass me a stone," he shouted.

I dropped my pole, picked up the biggest stone I could find and ran over to him with it. He took it and brought it down as hard as he could on the fish's head.

I stood up to my ankles in the river mud and watched. Any thoughts I'd had about Steppin being delicate vanished as I watched him bashing the fish. I wondered if grownups had ever seen him like this, pounding away with his hair falling over his eyes and his new clothes getting all wet.

At last he stood up. The fish was dead. "Th.. thanks," I said.

"It's a big one. Pity we haven't got a fire," Steppin said, raising his hand to hit it once more for luck. "Shit!" he suddenly shouted, another surprise. Pa would tan my hide if I ever spoke like that.

"What's the matter?" I asked.

He shook his hand and blew on his forefinger.

"Let me s.. see," I said, trying to get hold of his hand, but he pulled it away.

"It's nothing. Just bashed my finger," he said.

"Let me see," I repeated, this time managing to take his hand and examine his finger.

"It's nothing, Mickey, honest," he said as I tried to find the injury. There was nothing to see, except his long, thin, pale fingers. But I wasn't really paying attention to them. It was him I wanted to look at, to see what he was like up close, without being obvious about it.

"It's nothing, Mickey. Really," he said, pulling his hand away and walking out of the water. I stepped back, dumbstruck by my own stupidity. Had he read my mind? Or just read my face as I looked at his hand? Then I thought maybe he reacted that way because everyone fussed over him like that. He must have hated it.

"You're right. It's n.. nothing," I said, watching him as he sat on the bank and started to gut the fish with a knife he pulled out of his pocket. "It may s.. swell later," I added in case he thought there was something funny about the way I'd looked at him.

He wasn't looking at me. He didn't want to speak to me. He didn't want me around. It was my fault for fussing in the first place. I shouldn't have let him see what I was thinking. I'd been stupid, like always.

Things had been going so well up to now. I had thought we were becoming friends. I was wrong. I'd lost him. He was going to finish gutting the fish and pick up his pole and go off back home and leave me.

He must know, I suddenly thought. My head became all dizzy and I couldn't see straight. He knew! He knew all about me. All the nightmares came back, like a flood. All the feelings I'd forgotten were boiling up inside me.

"What's the matter?" Steppin said, looking up, when I started sobbing like I always did when I remembered. I tried real hard to stop myself. I couldn't let him see me like this. Not here, not anywhere.

"N.. n.. nothin'," I said, though it didn't come out right. I wasn't feeling good. I clenched my fists and tried not to move, but the world around me was swaying from side to side. I felt sick but I kept my mouth shut.

"Mickey, what's the matter?" Steppin asked again, looking worried.

I turned away, so he couldn't see me. "Nothin'. N.. nothin's wrong," I said, trying to make my voice sound normal. "Nothin's wrong." That sounded better. I couldn't let him see me the way I sometimes got.

I turned back and saw him shrug his shoulders. He finished threading a string through the fish's mouth and held it up to show me, dangling on the end.

"Got to catch some more," he said.

I didn't say anything. He knew. Here by the river. Of all the places to feel bad, this was the last. Up to now I had kept this place special. If I could feel bad here, it wasn't special any more.

Steppin was holding his fishing pole, his hook freshly baited with a new worm, smiling as if nothing had happened.

He hadn't rejected my friendship after all. I had another chance. This time I wouldn't blow it. I baited my hook and went to join him by the water's edge. He cast his line a little way out. I did the same and then we waited.

Time passed, but no more fish were biting. We didn't say much to each other. I didn't have anything to say and Steppin seemed happy like that. Then the sun got real high and Steppin said he'd better get home for lunch. He pulled his line from the water and began twisting it round the pole.

Then I had an idea. It kind of scared me, but I said it anyway. "Why d.. don't you come back to m.. my place for lunch?" That way he could meet Ma again, and if Ma liked him, maybe she could talk to Pa. Then things might get a little easier.

"Sure," Steppin said, "if your Ma doesn't mind."

I thought about the way she'd shouted after me when I'd gone to pick up the rod. She wasn't really mad. Besides, she wouldn't shout in front of Steppin.

I shook my head. "N.. no, she won't," I said, hoping it was true. "Come on." We picked up our rods and, Steppin still carrying the fish I'd caught, scrambled up the riverbank.

Rules

The tractor had broken down again. "What did I tell you, boy?" Pa shouted at me from the kitchen door.

Steppin and I were walking up the path. The first I knew Pa was back was when I heard his voice. My heart sank. Steppin looked at me. "I'll wait in the barn," he said. He ran off as if he was on his way home. I walked up to the house, wishing I was anywhere else but here.

"What did I tell you, boy?" Pa repeated as I got up close to him. "Get in," he said and followed me into the kitchen. "I told you, didn't I?" he said, leaning over me.

"B.. but Pa ...?" I said, pleading with him. It wasn't fair.

"Mickey, I told you something, didn't I, a long time ago, which you have obviously forgotten." He leant down even closer so that his face was almost touching mine. I reckoned he was getting close to hitting me. Not that I didn't deserve it, defying him like I had.

Pa had told me often enough the things I could and couldn't do. Bringing other kids back to the house was one. Going off the farm was another. Even on the farm there were places I couldn't go.

He didn't want me to have any friends after he took me away from that place, not until I "behaved", he said. The word had got around. None of the boys from the other farms came over now.

"Steppin's new," I said. "His folks just moved into the old Parker place. I thought he could come for lunch."

"Steppin? What kind of name is that?"

"That's his name."

"What's his real name?"

"I don't know!" I said, shaking my head and shouting at my boots. "He said it was his name." Even if I had known Steppin's real name, I wouldn't have said it. It would make him ordinary, and I didn't want that.

"What did I tell you about other kids, boy? Something that's up to you, right? What did I tell you?"

"P.. pa ..." I started pleading again, feeling tears well up in my eyes.

"What did I tell you?"

He wasn't going to hit me, but I wished he would, just to get it over with.

"N.. no kids is allowed to come here, to play with me on the farm, till I go b.. back, go b.. back... to..."

"Go back where?"

I couldn't say it.

"Go back where?" He wasn't shouting. He was just quiet, waiting for me to say the word he wanted to hear.

I knew he'd make me say it. He'd make me stand here all afternoon, if need be. It was all part of him trying to "re-educate me", till I was fit to be with other folks again.

"B.. b.. back to..." I whispered the word, hating my father for making me say it.

I hated that place. I hated him. Wasn't it enough chasing away Steppin? Why did he want to hurt me more? I was pretty sure that he liked being cruel to me and liked making me repeat my rules.

"Back where?" Pa asked, pretending he hadn't heard.

I could feel tears running down my cheeks. I hated him. All I wanted was Steppin to come in for lunch. It wasn't going to hurt anyone. Ma hadn't minded. Why should Pa? Instead he was going on and on about the place I really hated.

I'd said it once. I wasn't going to say the word again. I won't, I won't, I told myself.

"Frank, don't be so hard on him." Ma had come in and was laying the kitchen table for lunch. I saw she'd put some aside in a paper bag for me. When Pa was in for lunch, I ate out if I could.

"He said it once. Just let it be," she added.

"Can't Steppin come in for lunch?" I begged, hoping to change the subject. "Please? He's our n.. new neighbor."

It didn't work. My father straightened up. "I told you once, boy. No." He pulled out a chair and sat down at the table as I stood there, the tears streaming down my face. Oh Pa, I thought.

"That boy will never learn," Pa said to Ma as if I wasn't there. "He can't do what he's told. He's got no sense at all. Can't even help about the farm. He don't even know what day of the week it is."

"Mickey's just fine," Ma said, quietly serving Pa his soup. She'd heard Pa go on like this before. So had I. "Anyway, he's your son!"

"I know he's my son. But he probably gets his empty head from your side."

"Frank!"

"Look at your Uncle Josh," Pa went on. "He was just as stupid. The boy probably got it from your mother too! They had to lock her up, didn't they?"

"My mother got TB, and they didn't lock her up neither! Frank, you're a cruel man sometimes. My Uncle Josh was not stupid, just slow, that's all. And they never locked him up."

"All your family's stupid or loony, just like the boy."

"Why did you marry me then?" Ma asked.

Pa look her straight in the eye. "I don't rightly know. Maybe then I didn't know too much about your kinfolk. It was too late to do anything about it after we were wed."

"Oh, Frank!" Ma burst into tears and ran out of the kitchen and up the stairs. Pa turned back to his meal. "You still standin' there, boy?" he asked, as he picked up his paper.

I grabbed my lunch bag and turned and ran out the kitchen. At the screen door I stopped and shouted back at my Pa: "You're so mean! I hate you! I hate you! I'll never speak to you again!" Then I slammed the door open and ran across the yard to the barn.

I didn't think Pa would let me back inside the house ever again, after what I screamed at him. I didn't care, I told myself. I just didn't care. Now I knew what my Pa really thought about me. I felt real mad and sad all inside. I wished he was dead.

I ran into the barn, hoping Steppin would be waiting for me. He'd caused me enough trouble, first with my Ma, now with my Pa. It wasn't fair.

Steppin was waiting in the barn, like he said, sitting on a straw bale at the other end by the open doors. I suppose he could tell from the way I looked that I hadn't been able to make Pa change his mind. I didn't want him to know what Pa had said so I didn't speak.

"No go?" he asked. I shook my head and carried on walking through the open doors. I was going to go straight back to the river. I told myself I didn't even care if Steppin didn't follow me. He was the one who started it all, just by being there. He could go to... hell for all I cared.

I knew that wasn't really what I thought.

Steppin followed me slowly, a few paces behind. I thought about turning on him and shouting at him to go away, or doing something even worse to make him feel what I felt right at that moment. Couldn't he see what trouble he had caused me? I'd only known him a day and I'd ended up crying, just like what happened with all the other kids. I hated him too.

"We could get lunch at my place instead," Steppin said quietly to my back.

I thought about it. It wasn't the same as taking him home. I wanted Pa and Ma both to welcome Steppin into our house! It wasn't fair that I couldn't have any friends.

I stopped and turned, wiping my hand over my face and scrubbing away the tears. I raised the paper bag I held in my hand. "I've got s.. something to eat here. My Ma made it. Want to sh.. share?"

"Sure," he said.

We sat by the path eating the sandwiches and not saying much. I kept thinking, why did Pa have to be so horrible and mean to me? I wondered if Steppin's Pa was cruel, like mine. I was real sorry for him, if he was. But somehow I didn't think he was.

Then we went back to the river and set up our fishing poles. I didn't bait mine. I was still angry and I didn't want to waste time digging up more worms. I just sat watching my wooden float twitching about in the water, as if the fish were playing with it, telling me they didn't need any bait to draw them to the hook. Maybe I could catch fish without any bait at all.

After a while Steppin caught a fish, but it escaped. After that, he didn't bait his hook either, but just sat there staring out at the river, watching it flowing past.

As my anger settled down to just simmering, I again began to spy on Steppin out of the corner of my right eye. I was trying to see if he wasn't as beautiful as I had originally thought yesterday after all.

I could have said handsome. But that didn't seem to fit at all. Besides, I liked beautiful better. I didn't see anything wrong with just thinking the word when I looked at him. To call him that would be different.

He didn't grow uglier the more I looked at him. The complete opposite happened. He became more and more beautiful.

He caught me staring at him and I quickly looked away. I thought that he must really get fed up of people doing that, which was why he covered his head with its long fine hair and shaded his face with the baseball cap. I felt rotten, doing the same as everyone else must do to him.

"Sorry," I said, looking at the river. "I didn't mean to stare at you."

"It's alright. I get used to it," he said, like it happened every day.

It must have been early evening when we decided to give up and go home. We'd done nothing but stare at the river all afternoon.

We walked back to the edge of his land. I said goodbye to him at the bit where he said his Pa was going to make a large square of front garden for his Ma. It was already staked out with string and pegs.

"Doin' anything t.. tomorrow?" I asked, casually, expecting him to say yes. He'd be busy or have some other excuse not to come out. I wasn't the kind of friend he could depend on, what with lunch being cancelled and all.

"Nothing special. Let's meet after breakfast, down by the river." He was smiling again.

"Okay," I said and suddenly everything was alright again. "After breakfast?" I asked.

He nodded. "Great!"

3

Town

Want to go into town?" Steppin asked as we met at the river. "My Pa gave me my allowance this morning."

"I.. I can't."

"How come? It's only a couple of miles, Pa says."

It wasn't the distance stopping me from going into town. I'd been there often enough. But what could I tell Steppin? Maybe it would be easier to go than trying to explain to him why I couldn't.

"All right then," I said, changing my mind. It was against the rules, but if I was with Steppin I might as well get hung for a cow as for a sheep.

Going into town was going to be a real big fat cow!

The dirt track shimmered in the heat ahead of us, making our journey more like that of a desert epic than the short distance into town. As we walked, I imagined that we were struggling through miles of shifting sands, the sun beating down, our bodies staggering from one sand dune to another — just as in story books.

While we struggled against the blazing heat of the desert, we talked. Steppin explained all about his Pa's buying the old Parker place. His mother hadn't wanted to, but, Steppin said, she was okay about it now, because they were near a town and would soon get to know people.

He explained that his Pa was fed up working for other people, doing the dirty jobs around their farms, so he decided to try it for himself to see if he could make it.

"He reckons getting covered in shit for yourself is different," Steppin said. It was funny to hear a boy as beautiful as him using a word like that.

"I s.. see," I said, not really interested in why his Pa moved his family into the old Parker place, just glad that I got to meet Steppin. But I didn't want him to stop, and figuring that he liked to talk about his Pa, I kept nodding and asking questions.

"Why the old P.. Parker place? It's been empty since before I was born, going on thirteen years." That was one number I did know. My age.

"It was cheap, so Pa says."

"It sh.. should be. No one has s.. set foot to p.. plough on that land in years." It was a saying I had either heard, or invented myself on the spot, spontaneous like. I didn't care. I liked the thought of saying it, so I did.

"It's full of weeds, so my Pa says." That was just what my own Pa had always said about the Parker place. He reckoned it would take a lot of work to make the place right. Moving in during the middle of a drought was plain stupid. It could ruin a man, he said.

I didn't tell Steppin what my father thought. I wanted his Pa to make it work.

"My Pa's got a strong pair of hands. We've got a new tractor coming –– a gigantic one, which will plough the whole farm in a week, so the salesman promised."

Steppin, to his great credit, defended his father from every slight that had been hinted at in our conversation. Not that I was trying to put his father down. Steppin was just anticipating me.

He must have heard all the arguments against his father's buying the run-down farm and his plans for it, from a lot of people, and he naturally sided with him, as any good son does.

"That's good," I said. "It'll be neat to see the fields growing." I tried to make him feel good in case I'd hurt him by making him think his Pa had made a mistake moving in to the Parker place.

"Once the fields are ploughed," Steppin went on, "then the winter crops can be sown, and next spring we'll get a huge harvest."

It sounded like he was repeating the words his father had probably used on his Ma to persuade her to move in. The house needed repairing after so many years, and a lot of cleaning. No one could hide that from Steppin's Ma.

"And as soon as he can, he's going to hire in people to help him -- provided he gets the bank loan," Steppin said, continuing to explain as we walked towards town.

"H.. how come you ain't working?" I asked.

"Pa doesn't want me to work all the time. He wants me to study hard. Except in summer. He says I should be out getting to know people, getting to know the town."

I really liked the sound of that. I wished my Pa was like that.

"My P.. Pa don't want me to help either," I said. "He says I'm too d.. dumb."

"That's crazy. You're not dumb."

Steppin was the first person to say something like that to me.

"I know I'm not d.. dumb. I'm just a little s.. slow sometimes. And Pa and the others don't like that."

"What others?"

"J.. just others."

Steppin could see I didn't want to talk about it, so he didn't say anything. Besides, we were almost in town. My stomach was already twisting into knots, because I could see through the dust the same buildings I hadn't seen for weeks

The road into town was straight, and led right up to the town square, to the bandstand in the middle of a square of trees. Those trees would need lots of water, I thought. They were still green, despite the drought. I knew the town council had its civic duties to perform. Watering the trees around the bandstand was one of them.

Then I got scared looking at the town and dropped my head. I thought if I could only see the dusty road in front of me, maybe the town wouldn't be so bad.

Then I saw someone. "Quick," I cried to Steppin, grabbing his thin wrist and pulling him off the road. I was too quick for him to think about resisting, and he let me drag him round the back of the gas station.

It was the first building this side of town. I led Steppin further along the fence round the station yard. It was rickety and the paint was falling off. I reckoned the owner had done nothing to it since it had been put up.

"Get down, quick. He'll see us," I hissed at Steppin, pulling on his wrist to make him get down on his knees, like me. I was desperate not to be seen.

"Who will?" Steppin asked as he got down beside me.

It was a natural question that I didn't want to answer. But I had to say something.

"N.. no one... important."

Steppin gave me a weird look and started to ask me another question.

"Shush," I said, clamping my hand over his mouth, and pulling him down until I was holding him against my chest, my other arm and hand around his chest in a really tight grip. I was a really strong kid, much stronger than Steppin.

Through the gaps in the fence I could see the owner of the gas station with his faded denim overalls and his greasy, balding head. He was standing by the pumps looking up and down the road for any sign of customers.

When he didn't see any, he stretched, like a dumb old cat not really thinking about what he was doing. Then he headed back indoors to where the fan was probably going full blast.

No wonder he was fat, I thought. He was lazy and I was sure he drank too much beer.

I wasn't dumb, I thought. For a kid my age, I was pretty good at judging people.

Realizing that I was still holding Steppin and had my hand clamped over his mouth, I let him go. My fingers had left a pink impression under his nose and on his chin, just below his red lips. My hand was wet where he had tried to poke his tongue out, to make me let go. He hadn't done what I would have in the same circumstances, if someone had wrestled me to the ground and forced my mouth shut. I would have bit them or elbowed them in the belly. Steppin had just waited for me to release him.

Sure the gas station owner couldn't see me, I stood up and leant back against the fence. It was supposed to be painted white like the town council wanted, but it flaked blue as I slid down to sit on my haunches.

I was so relieved that the station owner hadn't seen me. I wiped Steppin's spit off my hand, onto the knee of my overalls.

"Phew! S.. sorry about that, Steppin," I said, looking up at him standing beside me.

"What's the matter, Mickey? Who is that man? What're you afraid of him for?" he asked. He looked over the fence, but there was no one there, then looked down at me again.

"Me? Afraid? I'm not afraid of n.. no one or n.. nothin' ... certainly not him!" I said, but I was looking at my boots more than at Steppin.

I didn't want him to see my face. I was real mad at him for saying that. I waited till I'd calmed down before I looked at him again.

"But..." Steppin said, sitting down next to me, not knowing what was going on and why I was behaving so strange. "But why did you drag me round here then?"

"I'm just being careful," I said, trying to think of something that would make sense to him. "He m.. might have told us to get out of here. He's had a lot of kids causing t.. trouble."

"What kind of trouble?"

Ouch! "J.. just trouble," I said.

That seemed to satisfy him.

"Come on," I said as I stood up, glancing back to see that it was clear. "Let's go." I didn't want Steppin to ask another question I didn't want to answer.

He followed me as I ran along the tattered fence, behind the gas station and up the short alley between the station and the next building. When I thought he was being too slow, I grabbed his wrist and dragged him past some garden fences and behind various bushes, trash cans and garages. Each time I thought I saw someone who might see us, I pulled him off the street. All the while I was still trying to reach the center of town without being spotted.

I felt like a rattlesnake, writhing and wriggling along the ground as we made our way into town, afraid of getting my head shot off by some cowboy with a Winchester. Bang – – you're history, rattler!

It wasn't surprising Steppin soon got a little fed up.

"Mickey! Stop it, will you?"

"S.. stop what?" I asked, looking back over a fence to check if we had been seen. Good, we hadn't.

"Look, Mickey, what's wrong?" he asked.

"Nothin', Steppin. N.. nothin's wrong."

"No? Well, come on then," he said. It was his turn to take my wrist and drag me along, out into the open and on to the street, right where we could be seen by everyone who was passing.

We were heading for the Five & Dime and I was in no hurry to get there. I dragged my feet, wishing I'd said no when Steppin had suggested we come into town, but there was nothing I could do about it now.

Steppin's fair hair swished to and fro as he walked backward, making sure I was coming along behind him as he led the way up Main Street. He wasn't stronger than me, but he was determined to make me go with him and I was afraid if I didn't go with him, he'd leave me. So I bowed to the inevitable and finally walked normally with him, thinking that if anyone saw us together, they might not recognize me. They would look at Steppin, not me, him being the beauty of the pair of us. I hoped that was what would happen, anyway.

"Why were we hiding like that back there?" Steppin asked.

I would have told him the truth if I thought he wouldn't have been horrified, and leave me standing in the middle of town to go off home, rejected by the one person I thought was going to be my friend.

He saw the way I looked as I tried to think what to tell him.

"Come on, let's get some jellybeans," he said, finally giving up on trying to get an answer. Just like most people did.

The Five & Dime. I didn't want to go in, but I didn't see what else I could do.

Five & Dime

Steppin pulled me across the porch and tried to push me inside the store ahead of him. I chickened out and pulled him back in front of me, shaking my head.

Then I looked through the door and saw someone coming toward us from inside. I knew right away who it was. I quickly pulled Steppin out of the way and behind a big apple barrel standing on the porch.

"What's the matter now?" Steppin wanted to know. I reckoned he was mighty fed up of me pulling him this ways and that, but I had to stop Her seeing us.

"Oh God! It's the W.. Widow Vanden!" I hissed, ducking down behind the barrel. "Wh.. whatever you do, d.. don't look at her eyes!"

Steppin crouched down with me and we looked down at the boards of the sidewalk when she came out. I was scared of being seen in town, but not half as scared as I was of the Widow Vanden. No one had ever seen her husband and everyone reckoned she was a witch.

"Come along, boy. Hurry up!" we heard her shouting to someone. I sneaked a peek and saw it was the grocer kid, Jimmy Johnson. His Pa owned the store. The kid had it made, I reckoned. All the sweets he could eat were his for the taking.

"Boys! Always expecting tips," the Widow was saying as Jimmy followed her to her truck. She turned on him lagging behind. "In my day, all we had was a thank you. Now, you want tips! What for, I ask. Just doing your job as you should."

Jimmy said nothing.

We watched as Jimmy dumped the Widow's groceries in the back of her truck. It was the only way he could get his own back on her for what she was saying.

"Mind them sacks of flour!" she near screamed at him. He backed off as she wagged her finger at him. I pulled Steppin closer, out of what I thought was her witching range.

"I'll have two extra for each one of them from your Pa, if any are split. One for my money and one for my trouble!"

I almost laughed when all Jimmy said was, "Yes ma'am." I knew what he was thinking.

"Well, don't just stand there. Get in!" she said.

"In?" Jimmy asked, taking another step back as he dusted his hands off on his white apron. He was real scrawny-looking and had his hair parted in the middle like his Pa did, greased down slick.

"Yes, in," she said, opening the door of the truck. "Unless you's expecting me to lug them heavy groceries from my truck to inside my place, are you?"

"Oh n.. no, she's going to..." I gasped.

"What?" Steppin asked.

I couldn't tell him straight out. I had to whisper what the Widow did to boys she got hold of. Steppin's face went pale.

Jimmy knew about the Widow's reputation too. He looked real scared. Still, he got into her truck and she drove off.

"Is she really going to do that?" Steppin asked as we stood up.

I nodded. "She's really a witch. She needs it for her spells!"

"Poor kid," Steppin said, holding his hand over his jeans like it was happening to him. "He'll never make it back to town like that."

He'd have to. He'd have to walk the mile or so back to the store afterwards. If he could still walk, that was.

Steppin opened the door and I followed him in. What with watching Jimmy Johnson, I'd forgotten I didn't want to come in here. Then I recognized the face behind the counter where the jellybean jar and all the other candies stood.

"Hello, boys," Mr Johnson said as we walked in. It was the same smile he gave all the kids, like he was their Pa, except we all knew he wasn't our Pa. All he wanted was our money.

He'd just finished tying on a clean white apron. Jimmy had said that his Pa changed his apron at least twice a day. He thought it gave customers a good impression and made them buy more things.

I hung around the back, hoping Mr Johnson wouldn't notice me, as Steppin walked up to the counter.

"I haven't seen you before, have I?" he asked Steppin.

"No, sir," Steppin said. "I just moved in with my folks to the old Parker place."

"I heard someone had bought it. I hope it goes well for you. Now, what would you like?"

Steppin smiled and swished his long fair hair to the side to clear his view. "Two quarters' worth of jellybeans, please."

Mr Johnson, still smiling, reached for the jar and dipped his hand in to retrieve the scoop. Then he noticed just who it was standing a little way behind Steppin, almost in the middle of the shop, both hands out in front, in plain sight.

I was more harmless that way.

I stood my ground, despite feeling I should run right out of the shop as he looked me over.

"Haven't seen you for a while, boy," he said to me.

"No sir," I said, staring at the spectacles on his fat face as we both remembered the last time I visited his shop. Then as he looked at Steppin, then back at me, I heard Steppin say: "It's okay sir, I'm paying for Mickey's," as he opened his hand to reveal the money. I knew he had misunderstood the way Mr Johnson had looked at me.

Mr Johnson looked hard at the money in Steppin's hand. I looked down at my boots as I heard Steppin explain to Mr Johnson that I didn't get an allowance from my Pa.

That was how I'd explained the lack of even one cent in any of the pockets of my overalls as we walked into town, when Steppin talked about spending the fifty cents given to him by his Pa that was burning a hole in his jeans pocket.

He went on and on about what he could spend the money on, until I thought I'd take the coins out of his pocket, stuff them up his nostrils, and then ask him how he would spend it?

"He doesn't get his allowance," Steppin went on. "His Pa's saving it for a bike for him." That's what I'd told Steppin, because he kept on about allowances and spending and the like. It was a lie, but I was used to telling lies about myself.

"All of it?" Steppin had said, when I told him how much I got a month, another invention of mine. "All five dollars?"

"Yep," I said. I had plucked the figure out of the air, and the purpose of saving it, trying to impress him with the richness of our farm and family.

Mr Johnson knew my Pa wasn't doing any such thing. He knew I'd never had an allowance. I pleaded silently with Mr Johnson not to say anything to Steppin about me and him and what happened in his store, or about my allowance or any of the other stuff he knew about me. I was lucky. He didn't say a word.

Two quarters' worth of jellybeans were served up from the jar and wrapped in a paper corner, with a scrunch and a twist from his big hands. Hands that had once reached for my collar as I ran from his shop trying to escape his clutches.

Mr Johnson came around to our side of the counter when he had firmly replaced the lid on the jellybean jar and followed us both out of the door. Only he and I knew why he did that. I saw his smile drop as he caught me watching his eyes.

I kept my hands together, fingers entwined as I left the shop, knowing that he was watching me even as he was smiling at Steppin.

"Bye, boys," he said, standing on the stoop. "Be careful."

I knew the last remark was meant for Steppin, who had thanked him politely, as he was obviously taught to do, beaming one of his innocent, angelic, smiles before he left the shop. I wanted to stop him doing that. I thought he shouldn't waste his nice smiles on anyone, especially not on Mr Johnson.

I could feel Mr Johnson's little eyes peering through his thick round glasses as he watched us, me in particular, walk toward the bandstand for some shade from the blazing sun.

Bandstand

I told Steppin that it would be cooler by the bandstand, being in the corner of the copse of trees that surrounded the square. The bandstand was the town's pride and joy, since it was the only one this side of the county.

"It's got a water tap," I said, knowing it was one of the few places where we could both slake our thirst and not get stared at.

Steppin drank first. Taking my kerchief out of the big pocket on the front of my overalls, I wiped the sweat off my forehead and the back of my neck, and out from under my armpits, pausing to rinse it out under the tap. The sweat that I rinsed down the drain wasn't just from the long walk in the sun. I finally wrung it out before tying it around my neck.

I then drank deeply of the running tap, feeling my belly swell with water, before joining Steppin in the shade around the other side, where he squatted with his back against the base of the bandstand. We ate some of the jellybeans, sucking on them and munching slowly. Well, I did anyway.

They were the first I had had in a long time, and I wanted to savor the delicious taste of all the different flavors, because

I knew it would be a long time before I would have jellybeans again.

Steppin was probably used to having them all the time, I thought. He was lucky to have parents like he did.

I looked at Steppin, to find him watching me with a puzzled, inquisitive look on his face. My heart sank again. I knew he was going to ask me about it all.

"Why did Mr Johnson look at you that way? Why didn't you come right up to the counter with me? Mickey, what're you scared of him for?"

I cooled my temper which had flared suddenly as he asked me each question. He was trying not to be angry himself. He was an inquisitive boy.

Not knowing the answers to things must really hurt him bad, inside. That was why he probably knew so much about everything, because his parents would tell him, rather than hurt him by saying no, like my Pa always did.

"I... it... He..." I didn't know how to start. Seeing Steppin staring at me, waiting to hear me tell the story, I knew I had to make sure he really understood what happened. So I stopped and I started again.

"Once I didn't pay for something from Mr Johnson's store."

"You stole it?"

"No!" I said. "I didn't steal it. I didn't mean to. I just forgot to pay!"

I remembered the fuss Mr Johnson made when he caught hold of me. He had dragged me through town to the sheriff's office. Everyone stared at us, especially at me. At the sheriff's office Mr Johnson had handed me over like I was some big criminal. I suppose I was, in their eyes.

Pa was called from the fields and came into town in the truck to collect me. He paid for the candy, and some more to compensate Mr Johnson for his trouble. He never spoke to me while he drove me home, but he tanned me hard when we got in the house.

Now Steppin thinking I stole gave me the same feeling I had that day in the middle of the street and in the sheriff's office.

"What did you take?"

"J.. just some candy," I said, without thinking.

Because I had told him everything, even though I hadn't wanted to, my face got red and I turned away from him. I hated him. He'd caught me. He knew everything about me. He knew I lied and I stole.

"That's all right, then. Want a bar?" Steppin asked, bringing out two bars of candy from the righthand pocket of his jeans.

I hadn't heard him order the candy from Mr Johnson, or pay for it. He must have...

Stolen it!

"H.. how? When...?" I asked, my hand reaching out for, but not quite touching, the hot candy.

He deepened his voice into that of a low-down gangster. "Better for you not to know, kid. The Feds might torture you!"

It was so funny I laughed. I was relieved that he wasn't going to leave me sitting there because he knew what I'd done in Mr Johnson's store. I elbowed him, trying to be real friendly-like, and he fell on his side onto the thick green grass before he could put his hand out to stop himself.

I giggled as he tried to get up, even though he was still squatting on his haunches. I pretended to help him back up by tugging his arm, but at the same time I pushed him over again.

"Stop it Mickey," he said, giggling and laughing as he fell back against the bandstand again. "You'll make me choke," he said as he bit into the candy bar. Finally I let him sit up again.

He didn't seem to mind me fooling about with him. He pushed me when he thought I wasn't paying attention, but I was ready for him and didn't fall over. Not the first time he pushed anyway. All the time he was trying to finish his candy bar, as if he had to make it disappear as quickly as he could.

We stopped messing about, and I tore the wrapper off my own bar, intent on eating it quickly before Mr Johnson counted all his candy and found two bars missing.

I knew that with Steppin's innocent looks, Mr Johnson wouldn't think it was him. That left only one person. He had me in plain sight all the while I was in his shop and he could see I hadn't taken anything. But I knew that wouldn't matter to Mr Johnson. Once a thief, always a thief, as far as he was concerned.

"We'd better get going. We'll be late for lunch," I said. It wasn't true, but I wanted to get out of town quickly before anyone else saw me and told my Pa. I stuffed the wrapper into the front pocket of my overalls, which was the deepest one I had, and taking Steppin's candy bar out of his hands, took the wrapper off and stuffed that in my pocket too.

"Evidence," I said to Steppin as he wondered what I was doing. I also stuffed my remaining jellybeans into the front pocket, hiding the candy wrappers. I would savor a few later. Steppin could afford to eat all of his up then and there. He could get more. I couldn't.

We drank from the tap once more, taking turns to swallow as much water as we could, to see us back home. I undid my kerchief, soaked it and tied it around my neck again.

Steppin splashed water on his neck and back. I could have done it for him, I thought. I could have used my kerchief to wipe his sweat away as well. Then I thought maybe he wouldn't like me touching him like that, so I didn't untie it.

I shuddered in the heat haze as Steppin and I started down the road again. Water from the kerchief tickled my skin as it ran down my back and front in dribbles, briefly cooling small streaks of my sweaty body, causing my skin to rise in goosebumps. It was sticking the hair under my arms, which had only just begun to grow.

Instead of sneaking out of town, like I'd made us do on the way in, we walked down the center of Main Street. Anyhow, there was no point in trying to hide. Mr Johnson would have told everyone he had seen me. And that I had been with the new kid from the Parker place.

As we got near the gas station, I held my head up high and walked right on past it, ignoring anyone who might be watching us go by. I thought if I didn't look, I wouldn't see them and maybe they wouldn't see me either.

As we passed the gas station, another trickle of water ran down my spine to the small of my back, where it was absorbed by my overalls before it could reach my butt. The trickle was very hot and I felt uncomfortable.

"I d.. don't care! You can't see me. I d.. don't care," my lips were repeating, unfortunately loud enough for Steppin to hear.

"What's that you're saying, Mickey?"

"Nothin'," I said, turning to him walking beside me. I shook my head. "N.. nothin', really."

"Is anyone lookin'?" I whispered a moment later, once we were past and kicking up the dust on the dirt road.

He looked round. "No, I can't see anyone," he whispered back.

"Good."

"What did you do to him, the gas station owner?" Steppin asked, as we headed over the rise in the road, just before I knew we would disappear from the view of anyone still looking at us from the gas station's dirty, dusty windows.

I shook my head, thinking that he kept asking a lot of questions I wouldn't answer. I didn't want to tell him, but especially not there, so close to the station.

Besides, it wasn't the owner I did it to. It was his son, which was even worse. His Pa had sworn he'd sort me out afterwards. So far, he hadn't. But he'd told my Pa and that had made my Pa even madder.

As we walked into the comforting summer haze away from the town that knew all about me, and I thought about certain bits of my past, I felt all hot and cold at the same time.

In the end, I reckoned there would be more than two people against me when it came right down to it. There'd be a line a mile long.

I shut my mind off from thinking about such things and looked down the road. I couldn't wait to get back to the river, so I could jump in and cool off properly, washing away all the sweaty dust we were kicking up around us and all the thoughts that kept on bothering me.

Lunch

Instead of going to the river, we went back to our homes to collect lunch. I knew mine would be inside a brown paper bag on the kitchen table where my Ma would put it for me.

Steppin said his lunch would be in a new lunch bucket, the kind with a lid. I didn't even have one of the old kind when I went to that place.

Steppin had a brown bottle in each of his hands as we met up. I had run after him, seeing him bouncing along as he walked on the way to the river. I just had my lunch bag and an empty canteen to dip in the river for water. My Ma insisted I should drink lots of water before I went out to the river again. She saw I'd been sweating a lot.

I didn't tell her why.

So I'd drunk lots of water from the kitchen tap, and fetched my tin canteen down from my room. I told her I would fill it up from the river when I got there. She must have seen the dust all over my overalls, but didn't say anything about where I might have collected it from.

"Want one?" Steppin asked, offering me one of the brown glass bottles.

"What is it?" The bottle was cold. I saw there was a layer of bubbles on top of the liquid inside.

"Pop. It's the best."

"Thanks."

I twisted the screw cap off and drank. I coughed as the bubbles fizzed and rose in my mouth and dribbled out of my nose.

Steppin laughed and pulled the bottle down a bit. "Take it easy, Mickey! Don't gulp it like that."

Licking my lips and wiping the fizz from under my nose, I laughed. "It's great." I didn't dare add that I really liked his laugh, too.

We sat on the riverbank, eating and drinking. I dipped the empty tin canteen into the river and stoppered it when it was full. It was there for both of us, I told Steppin.

"Thanks. Beats running back home."

The fizz from the pop made quite another impression on me, as I belched and farted at the same time.

"S.. s.. sorry..." I started to say, trying to be polite in company, but soon gave up as Steppin was already in fits of giggles.

Steppin collapsed altogether when he let out a big fart himself.

"Phew! That's a real stinker Steppin!" I complained. I thought he must have been saving it up for a long time.

"Yeah, I know," he said, waving his arm about to get rid of the smell. "It's one of my best talents, so my Pa says."

"Yeah?" I said. "Well... what about this one then?" I asked him, doing it again. It was my habit too, when I got up in the morning.

At least we had something in common.

It was one of the strangest competitions I had ever participated in, but great fun, seeing who could make the loudest and longest one.

"Want to go for a swim?" I suggested when we had both run out of gas and giggles and were lying back on the grass, soaking up the sun.

He looked up to see the river below us. I thought it was clearly inviting us to jump in the water, to wash away the grit and the sweat.

I was still itching from the dusty trip to town. It really irritated me.

"It's okay," I said, seeing him undecided. "The w.. water's not deep and I'm a good s.. swimmer. I won't let you d.. drown, if that's w.. what you're afraid of."

"I'm a good swimmer too," Steppin said defiantly as he started to undo his shirt buttons.

"There's a good place to bomb just here." I pointed to a place just in front of us. The bank was about five feet higher than the river and the water was deep enough that we wouldn't hurt ourselves on the river bed.

We took off all our clothes. Like I thought, Steppin was pale and skinny, but not too skinny. I was bigger than he was and browner, but he had just as much hair. I looked at him all naked like that and got a funny feeling inside, something I'd never felt before. It made me feel good and uncomfortable at the same time. Then I realized that part of me was beginning to grow and I got worried case Steppin saw it. But he was too busy running down to the riverbank, so I just followed him.

We stopped at the edge, then took a short step back and jumped into the water. I heard Steppin squealing as we dropped like two atom bombs. I squealed too as I pulled my knees up to my chest and closed my eyes just before I dropped in. The water was cool and fresh as I sank to the bottom.

Surfacing, I looked to see Steppin bob back up a couple of feet away. His face was covered by long wet hair. He pushed it back with his hand in a real nice way. It looked really good the way he did it, like he was kind of older than he really was.

"Great," he said. "Let's do it again."

"Okay."

We raced for the shore and climbed up the bank. Steppin was all wet and watching his pink butt gave me a funny feeling. Like I wanted to hold it and see what it felt like. Except I knew I couldn't. He'd think I was weird and wouldn't want to play with me again.

So we played all afternoon, bombing and swimming and lying on the grass. And each time I touched Steppin by mistake, I jumped back like I'd had an electric shock. But I couldn't understand why the shock felt so good.

4

Steppin's Pa

The next day I got up early, with the cockerel's last crows in my ears. Ma had just put out breakfast and Pa was sitting down to his. They were both surprised to see me, but said nothing to make me run back up to my room. They probably thought I'd got confused over the time.

I sat next to Pa, again surprising him into silence. He ate his breakfast while reading the paper. It saved time, I supposed, doing the two together.

I knew Pa worked really hard to make our farm a success, even in the drought, but sometimes I wished he would let me help. There were things even a kid as dumb as me could do. He just never trusted me to do anything. When there was a lot to do and he had the money, he preferred to hire someone else rather than use his own flesh and blood.

Ma sat down and poured herself some cereal. "What're you going to do today, Mickey?" she asked. It sounded as if she was being nice, not trying to trap me. She was still trying to make up for the way I'd felt the other day.

I looked up from eating — well, bolting — my food and spluttered "N.. nothin'" as I dipped my spoon back in the bowl.

"Don't speak with your mouth full and give your mother a civil answer!" Pa barked at me, making me nearly jump out of my skin. He looked as mean and angry as he always did.

I swallowed the cereal and looked back to Ma and said, "N.. nothin'. I'm doin' nothin' today, Ma."

Ma looked at me as if that was the wrong answer, but she didn't say anything, just got on with her own breakfast.

I finished my cereal and grabbed some bread and spread butter and jam over it as quickly as I could without upsetting either of them. As soon as I'd finished, I started to get up so I could go over and see Steppin .

"Where are you going, boy?" Pa asked. "You sit down and wait for this family to finish breakfast together before you go anywhere."

I almost did sit down. But my Ma said, "Leave him be, Frank," and so I just left the table. I knew Pa didn't care whether I sat watching him eat or not. If he wasn't telling me what to do, he was ignoring me. Well, I could ignore him like he ignored me.

"You washed yourself, Mickey?" Ma asked.

"Yeah, Ma. And b.. brushed my t.. teeth."

I'd washed my face and under my arms and round the back of my neck. I'd even opened the bathroom cabinet and taken the bottle of cologne which my Pa used. I'd opened it nervously, scared he was going to walk in any moment. It smelt good. I put a little on my cheeks. I thought maybe Steppin would smell it and like it.

"Remember the rules, boy," Pa said without looking up from his paper as I pushed open the screen door.

"Yeah, Pa," I said, trying to sound as though I meant it, so he wouldn't get suspicious.

Outside the sun was already high, announcing that it was going to be another burning hot, cloudless day. I quickly pulled off my blue flannel shirt, which I had previously carefully tucked in, and flung it on the porch seat.

Ma would find it and shake her head that I was getting too much sun, but I didn't care. I bet with myself many times that adults, if they really admitted it, would do anything to run around half naked, especially in the summer heat. All those sweaty clothes? Yeuch!

I picked up my fishing pole in the barn and ran most of the way over to Steppin's place, the heat of the sun already prickling my skin. I loved that feeling and the bright glare the sun gave off. Seen through squinting eyes, the sharp edges of the landscape kind of melted away. I liked it that way.

I forced myself to calm down, and slowed my run to a trot, then to a walk, as I approached the place where Steppin's front garden was going to be. I stopped, and then walked calmly up the dirt path to his door, trying to act as if I was just taking a casual stroll to visit a neighbor.

Before I knocked on the door, I quickly sniffed under my arms, not wanting my sweaty run to be noticed. They were all right. Then I wiped a finger across my cheeks, wanting to make sure the nice smell was still there. I sniffed the finger. It was.

Only when I saw the cause of the thump-thump-thump echoing in my ears, did I realize that I had made my hand into a fist and was banging repeatedly on the door.

I stopped my next blow.

"Hi, Mickey," Steppin said. "Ready?" he asked.

I let out all my breath in a forceful "Yes!"

He looked exactly like I'd seen him yesterday and the day before. The same long fair hair and green eyes and red lips. He had washed his hair, or his Ma had done it for him. Either way, it was all nice and shiny. His eyes sparkled, and his thick eyelashes blinked a couple of times as he looked at me standing on the step just in my boots and overalls.

I was really glad to see him. I think he could tell that from the way I was smiling at him. My heart start to pound again harder and harder as I stood looking at him.

"Okay," he said, "just let me get my fishing pole. Come on in," he added, stepping back to let me through the door.

He was being very polite, but I didn't want to move. His Ma might see me. She might see right into me and see what I'd been thinking as I stood out there on her porch. Then she'd be real keen to keep me away from her son.

"It's all right, come on in," Steppin said, thinking I was just being shy. I felt his hands pulling gently on the straps of my overalls, leading me over the doorstep and a little way into the kitchen.

His Ma wasn't around but the radio was on. Some man was talking political talk. It was a voice I'd heard before. "Who's th.. that on the radio?" I asked. It was the kind of thing I never asked at home in case it got Pa mad for some reason.

"It's the President," said Steppin. "Eisenhower," he went on when I couldn't remember the President's name. "He's running for election again."

"Oh," I said.

I must have looked bored, cause Steppin changed the subject. "Wait here. I'll get my pole."

He was back in a minute and we went out onto the porch.

He took off his shirt like I had done. But unlike me he folded his shirt neatly and left it on the porch bench. Then he took a tin of some cream out of his pocket and started smearing himself with it.

"Wh.. what's that for?" I asked.

"Suncream," he said. "I get burnt real easy. Mom makes me put it on."

I didn't say anything. I thought it was the kind of thing that only sissies did. But Steppin was no sissy.

He rubbed the cream all over his body, down to his belt. I got a funny feeling watching him.

"Can you put it on my back please, Mickey?" he asked. "Mom'll kill me if I get burnt."

My mouth was dry. I couldn't say anything, but I took the tin and lifted a gob out with my fingers. It was white and greasy as I rubbed it over his back.

"Ouch! Not so hard, Mickey," Steppin hollered.

"S.. sorry," I said, rubbing gentle and slow. It was difficult for me, cause I was kind of trembling and didn't want Steppin to notice it. But he didn't say anything, just moved his shoulders around a bit so I could spread the cream better.

"Thanks," he said, when I'd finished. "You want some?"

I was going to say yes, when someone came round the corner of the house. He was a tall man, younger than my Pa and with not so fierce eyes.

"Hi, Pop," said Steppin. "Pop, this is Mickey."

He was wearing a hat, but underneath it I could see that his face was as pale as Steppin's. He even looked like I thought Steppin would when he grew up. I stepped back, expecting the worst. Surely he could tell what I'd been thinking just by looking at me. But all he said was "Hi, son, good to meet you."

I tried to say something, but the words wouldn't come out.

"Mickey and me are going fishing," Steppin said.

"Enjoy yourselves," his Pa said. "You're Frank Robson's boy, aren't you son?" he turned to me.

"Yes, s.. sir," I said, really scared now. If he knew who I was, he must know about my Pa and my rules, mustn't he? So how come he didn't say anything, didn't tell me to get on home?

"Come on over anytime."

Before I could try to say anything, he'd walked into the house. I thought maybe he'd got it wrong, thought I was someone else. No one else treated me like that.

"Come on Mickey," Steppin said, wondering why I was just standing there. "Let's go." He grabbed my left hand and pulled me off the porch and onto the cracked and dusty soil that one day was going to be a flower garden. All the while I was wondering whether I should tell Steppin's Pa just who I was.

Steppin was obviously anxious to get to the river and the waiting fish, I thought, as my feet caught up with his quick pace. Before long we were running down the sloping dusty road that took us to my special path across my Pa's two bottom fields and down to the water.

Steppin let go of my hand as we were crossing the fields. It was real sweaty and greasy from the suncream, so I wiped it on my overalls and thought about the fact that it had rubbed all over Steppin's back. I sniffed it, but all I could smell was the sweet smell of the cream.

Not much grew in the bottom two fields. Pa said the soil was too poor to make it worth irrigating them. As we ran we kicked up the dust like a cavalry charge going to the rescue of the wagons surrounded by Indians. Except that there wasn't anyone who needed rescuing as we made it to the water's edge.

We dug some bait. Steppin handed me the largest mudworm he found. "You use it," he said. It was much bigger than any of the worms I'd dug up and I thought it was really good of him to give it to me.

"Thanks," I said. I slipped my hook through the worm twice.

"That's alright, Mickey. Anytime," he said smiling.

Just seeing that smile made me blush. I turned away to throw my line, wishing I could see that smile all the time.

The drought and the seemingly endless supply of sunshine which greeted me every morning as I pushed open the screen door made the days of my exile melt into one long summer's day. Now there were two of us to share its blazing glory, the sun seemed to shine ever more brightly, ever more golden.

Except in winter, when it was too cold, every time things were getting on top of me I had walked or run, almost every day, here to the river. My river. Big and wide and slow-moving, it seemed unaffected by the terrible drought that was devastating the land that it passed through. It was the one thing in life that I could trust, where I felt at home.

Screaming

"What're you thinking about, Mickey?" Steppin asked. We'd been sitting there for some time with nothing biting. He must have noticed I was staring at the bobbing float without even thinking there was a fish on the hook trying to get away.

"Nothin'," I said.

He was quiet for a bit. Then he asked a question I wasn't prepared for.

"Pop says you don't go..."

I couldn't help it. I dropped my fishing pole, put my hands over my ears, closed my eyes, and screamed.

"Don't you ever say that word! Never, ever again! Never! Never! Never! Never! Never! Never!!!!"

My head was hurting and I tried to shake it from side to side, to stop remembering everything, to stop the nightmares rushing back. This was the one place I'd never had them and now they were here and I was hurting and hurting and screaming and couldn't stop.

All the time my head was going round I wanted to be sick but there was nothing in my stomach to throw up. Suddenly, I felt Steppin grabbing me by the arms and shaking me. Or maybe I was the one shaking. I didn't know, but I heard him saying something as he tried to pull my hands away from my ears.

"Stop it, Mickey! Please, please stop it!"

I began screaming again, louder and longer. I felt his hand on my mouth, but it was open so wide that his fingers slipped inside. Without thinking, I closed my teeth and began to bite and only stopped when I realized what I was doing. I opened my eyes and then my mouth and watched him snatch his hand away.

He looked at me so strange, like he thought I was mental, that I began to be scared.

I started to cry. Tears burst out of my dazed eyes as I sobbed and sobbed and sobbed.

Steppin stood there, watching me. I had really frightened him. I had let him see all the nasty horrible things that went on inside me. Now he'd never want to speak to me again.

I was still crying and shaking as I turned away and fell on the grass. I didn't want him to see me and the way I had looked. I thought maybe if I could stop crying we could pretend it had never happened. But I knew that was impossible; he could never forget it.

Then I felt his hands on my shoulders trying to pull me gently up. I tried to shake him off but not too hard, because I didn't know if I wanted him to let go. All the time I kept my eyes closed because I didn't want to see him and I hoped he wasn't looking at someone as ugly and bad as me.

"What's wrong, Mickey? What's wrong?" he said over and over again.

What was he asking what was wrong for? Surely he knew. His Pa must have told him everything. That made me cry even more.

"Mickey, please stop, please..." He pulled me again but I wouldn't sit up.

But he sounded so unhappy that I stopped struggling against him. I opened my eyes and let him pull me up. I half looked at him, not wanting him to see the tears still running down my face.

I could tell he was shocked by what he saw. I wasn't surprised. Most people would be, if they saw me like I was then. He couldn't understand what was going on. His hands kept hold of me real tight, like he was afraid I was going to try and run away. His eyes were all open from the fright I was giving him. He was so close to me that if I leant forward, I could have...

Realizing what I was thinking, I stopped crying. But I couldn't stop thinking the thought. I closed my eyes but it was still there, as if I was really doing it.

"I'm s.. s.. sorry," I blurted out, shaking my head from side to side. "It's j.. just, it's just that I hate that place, I hate everything to do with it. I h.. hate them all."

"It's okay, Mickey. It's okay," he said. "I'm sorry. I didn't know."

I wasn't afraid he was going to ask me to explain, but he didn't. It didn't seem to matter to him. I was glad it was just him around when I went off my head. I don't know what his Ma or Pa would have done.

Steppin just looked at me. Maybe he saw something. Maybe he saw what I was feeling. But all he said was it was all right. We weren't going to talk about it any more. Everything would be all right.

I nodded my head. "I'm sorry, S.. Steppin."

As I calmed down and wiped away the tears from my blazing cheeks, I told myself I was alright. That Steppin didn't know any of my secrets. He couldn't know them.

I felt better as I looked into his eyes as he watched me change from a mental case back to... to whatever he thought of me that first day we met on the riverbank.

That made me like him even more. Anyone who could handle my fits could have my vote for President any day.

"I'm alright n..now," I said to him, even though it wasn't true. "I'm okay," I said, trying to smile.

He let go of my arms.

"Mickey! your fishing pole!" he suddenly cried. "It's gone!"

Maybe he wanted to put it into my hands, to bring me back to reality and take my mind off the fact that he had started my fit.

The news that my pole had gone made me forget everything that had just happened. I scrambled to my feet and ran to the water's edge. I couldn't see it anywhere. Then I remembered that just before I'd had my fit the float had been twitching and moving in the water, probably with a fish nibbling on the baited hook.

"There it is," he cried as he saw the pole floating in the river just a little downstream from where we had been sitting. "Quick!" he called out.

It had drifted into the riverbank but as we watched it began to move out again. The fish on the hook must have still been trying to shake itself free.

As I ran down to where it had got caught, it drifted back out into the current. I kicked off my boots and half dove, half jumped into the river, still in my overalls, knowing that to take them off would just be wasted time. Time I couldn't afford if I wasn't going to lose the pole forever.

I couldn't ask Pa to get me another one, especially the way I had been behaving lately. He'd probably get real mad at me just for losing this one. The only way Pa would agree to buy me another pole would be if I promised I'd go back to that place. And I'd never do that.

I couldn't swim properly in my overalls, but it was too late to get back to shore and pull them off. I just chased the pole as fast as I could, stretching my hand out to try and catch it. But it kept bobbing out of my reach as the current, or maybe the fish, pulled it away. For some reason I was thinking of how the fish felt, trying to shake itself free.

I tried again and reached the pole just as something was trying to pull it downward. My heart lifted as my fingers touched and then closed over it. It was trembling, like the fish at the other end was still trying to get away. Then I felt something snap and thought that maybe it had broken, which meant I had as good as lost it.

I was just thinking how mad Pa was going to be and how I wouldn't be able to fish again, when suddenly the whole length of the fishing pole floated up, unbroken. It had been the line that had broken, with the fish still on the hook. That meant I was all right. I wouldn't have to beg Pa for another, nor make a promise I wouldn't keep.

Steppin cheered as I stepped back onto the shore. Like I'd just won the Super Bowl, I held the fishing pole above my head, a broad smile on my face. "Well done," Steppin said. "I didn't know you could swim so good." That made me smile even more. I must have been good if he thought I was.

I was really happy to have the fishing pole. Not having it would have been the end of the world. What else could I do except fish and swim in my river? I couldn't swim all the time and without fishing I would have nothing to do except skip stones and sometimes even that got boring.

Which was why was I so grateful to Steppin. He had saved me twice in one day. From going completely mad and for making sure I rescued my pole. Even though I was soaking wet, he put his arms around me and joined in my exuberance. We were both jumping up and down with sheer joy, shouting as we did, many long and loud cheers.

"S.. Steppin! You're great!" I cried. "You were s.. so quick and you didn't m.. mind when I, when I... I'm s.. sorry about the w.. way I acted," I said.

"That's all right, Mickey. I wanted to help you," he said.

I didn't say anything else, but hugged him one more time. My heart was pounding and not just from jumping in the river to rescue my fishing pole.

"You're all wet," Steppin said, moving out of my reach, but he didn't sound mad. "You'd better take your overalls off before you catch cold."

"Here?" I said.

"Why not?" It was a good question. After all, there was no one to see and we'd both stripped off the day before.

I didn't like to tell him it gave me a funny feeling thinking of being naked in front of him.

"I'd b.. better not," I said. "They won't d.. dry proper here. I'll go home and change. My Ma would get mad if she found out I was wearing wet clothes. She'd be sure I'd catch something real bad."

"Okay," he said. "Are we going to carry on fishing afterwards?"

"I haven't got a line," I said.

"That's right. I forgot," he said. "Why don't you come over to my place after you change?"

I thought about my Pa and how mad he would get, but I didn't care. Then I remembered that Steppin's Pa had said I could come over any time. So that kind of made it all right. "Sure," I said.

We left our poles high on the bank where they wouldn't fall into the river. Then I picked up my boots and we made our way back up the trail across the dry fields, and over the crazed, sunbaked soil that took us back to the road. Then he walked up to his house, with the same light step he always walked, and I ran back to mine.

I was lucky. Both Ma and Pa were out. Ma must have been helping Pa in the field or maybe she'd gone into town. I ran up to my bedroom, pulled off my wet overalls and dried myself down. Then I pulled on my other pair, which Ma had washed the other day. I looked at myself in the mirror and saw what a mess my hair was. I tried to comb it, but it was taking too much time. So I ran back downstairs and headed off across the yard back to Steppin's place.

I hoped Ma wouldn't be back too soon, or if she did come back, she wouldn't find my wet overalls hanging out my bedroom window, the window jammed shut on the straps. In this hot sun they should dry in an hour or two.

Steppin was waiting outside his house, holding two bulging brown paper bags. He saw me, waved and headed towards me.

"Mom says we can have lunch in the barn," he said as I reached him. "Pop said to her that he thinks you're a bit shy." He smiled and poked my bare ribs with his elbow as we walked. "So Mom said you might be happier having lunch in the barn."

That was all right by me, but not for the reasons that Steppin's Ma and Pa thought.

The barn was very old but strong enough to last for years. Steppin pointed out the bits his Pa was going to repair. He'd already bought in some bales of straw to feed the cows. Then there'd be room for the feed he bought from the other farmers. In the winter there would be a stall for the cows. Just outside he'd already fixed up the old chicken coop for them to have fresh eggs in the morning. Next year he would store his own straw and the rest of the harvest.

It sounded as if Steppin's Pa knew what he was doing. I said that when the drought let up the harvest was bound to be bountiful, since the land had lain fallow for years. I liked the word bountiful. It was nice to say it and it meant such nice things, like overflowing and the like.

We climbed up to the hayloft and ate our lunch, swinging our legs over the edge. Lunch was real good. Steppin's Ma had given us sandwiches, home-made lemonade, apples and a big chunk of cheese.

Looking out of the window we could see Steppin's Pa already back in the fields ploughing with the new tractor. He was going to sow a late crop. I knew my Pa was going to help Steppin's Pa by lending him the pump to irrigate some of his fields as long as Steppin's Pa paid for the fuel. He'd told Ma about it at dinner last night. He thought Steppin's Pa wasn't going to get much of a crop, it being the wrong time of year, but, he said, a man should still help his neighbor. I wanted to say something about playing with Steppin but thought it wasn't a good idea. I should just carry on doing it until he found out.

Steppin and I spent the rest of the afternoon in the barn, making a fort out of some of the bales and playing cowboys and indians. Chasing each other around the old barn and just messing about with Steppin was more fun than I'd had in years, maybe as long as I'd lived.

It was more fun than hiding in our own loft, which was where I sometimes went when the world was especially mean to me or Pa belted me or went on about the place I never wanted to go to. When he finally left me alone, most times I would run out of the house and over to the barn. Sometimes I spent the whole night there. Ma always knew where I was but she never came over to see if I was all right.

Now I was with Steppin and everything was fine. I just wished it could always be like this.

5

That Place

After that, Steppin and I spent every day together. Some times we went down to the river, other times we wandered around his Pa's farm. It was fun, like it had been wandering around our farm until Pa got mad at me and told me he didn't want me around. It became another one of his rules.

At first I was scared what my Pa would do when he found out I was seeing Steppin every day. If he didn't see us in the fields, Steppin's Pa would surely tell him. I thought he'd tell me to stay home, but he never said anything to me and I never said anything to him. I guess Ma persuaded him that it would be all right for me to have one friend. I'm glad she did, otherwise I would have gone crazy on my own.

That day was the same as all the rest. The weather was perfect for doing pretty much nothing. The blue sky held our squinting gazes. It was hot and cloudless and the sun was already sweltering the bone-dry land.

As usual Steppin and I met outside his place right after breakfast, and started out without choosing any particular direction, but knowing we'd end up by the river or exploring the fields.

We took the precaution of taking our fishing poles, bait can and trowel everywhere we went, just in case we did end up at my river. Even if we didn't fish, they were safe enough in a secret place I had showed Steppin.

Steppin was holding the fishing poles as we walked along the dirt road toward the river. I could tell he wanted us to go there. I had the bait can and the trowel tied on a piece of string, slung over my well-tanned shoulder. I was also carrying the lunch and holding the strings of our lemonade bottles.

I still did not want to call it our river, even though we'd met there and been going there together for weeks. For one thing, most of it was on my Pa's land and second, inside me, I didn't want to share the only place I really thought I was safe.

Sharing things was not my strongest point. Being an only child, I was used to having things all to myself. It was difficult to see that to share was the best way to make friends.

I tried to be different with Steppin. I wanted to share other things with him, but not yet the river. I showed him all the secret places I knew on what was now his farm. It was good fun me showing him all these places he didn't know, which I'd used when I wanted to run away from the world and everything it felt about me. Then I thought maybe he'd found all these places by himself anyway, cause every kid always explores his new home. But he pretended like he didn't.

We'd caught a lot a fish in the past few days. I took half of them home to Ma. She cooked some, put some in the freezer and even sold some of the bigger ones to people in town. I don't know if she told them that I caught them. She never gave me any of the money. Sometimes I wondered why I went on catching fish if I didn't get paid for it.

Pa ate the fish all right, but never said a thing about where they came from. Neither did I. I just wanted to keep out of his way as much as possible.

Steppin's Ma sold some of his catch for him. He got the money and bought candy from Mr Johnson's store for both of us. I guess Mr Johnson didn't count the candy bars that day after all.

When we got to the river I dug for bait while Steppin put the lemonade in the water. That was the first thing we did every day when we went to the river, putting the bottles in the water and tying them to a branch so they wouldn't float away. When it came time to eat, we'd pull them out again and open the sandwich bags, taking out an apple and a sandwich each, placing the apples on the grass and then, biting at the same time, we would start into our sandwiches.

Steppin handed me the fishing poles and I placed them carefully on the grass bank beside me. I took my boots off, and with bait can and trowel in my hand, scrambled down to the mud to start digging.

"Got enough yet?" Steppin asked as I dug hard for bait to fill the can.

"Just about. Wh.. where's the lemonade?" I asked, looking up to see him coming over to join in my search for worms.

"Over there, tied to that tree," he said, pointing to where he had lowered the two bottles into the water. "They'll be cold by lunchtime," he added.

His hair suddenly caught the sun, making my heart pop and stomach gurgle. I got funny feelings like that every day since I met Steppin. I still couldn't believe that he and I were friends. That was why I hadn't told him anything about my past. I was afraid that if he knew about it he wouldn't want to be my friend any more.

"Great," I said, nodding at him. I could have said that I thought he was great too, but didn't dare. I didn't dare say anything I thought about him to his face, though I sometimes said it to myself when I was in bed at night. Before that, I would stand at the window of my room, watching his house until his bedroom lights went out. Then I would say goodnight to him before getting into bed myself and going to sleep.

We set up the poles and dipped the hooks gently into the river, as we had done for the past weeks. It was like everything was different here. I'd died and was living a different life, one filled with happiness and joy at finding friendship with Steppin.

But I couldn't help thinking about what would happen if he knew of my secrets. I knew he wanted to ask me, but he never did. He just waited for me to tell him, but I was never going to do that.

I knew what would happen if he knew. He'd think I was the worst monster he'd ever met. He'd run home, leaving me sitting on the riverbank all alone. He'd lock his bedroom door and swear never to see me again. He might even beg his parents to take him away from the farm to make sure we never met again.

If he did that, I would kill myself, I knew. I had even planned how to do it too. I would simply jump into the river with my boots on. As they pulled me down to the bottom I'd open my mouth suck in all the water and drown. I'd heard somewhere that drowning was easy. It didn't hurt. Even if it did hurt, it couldn't hurt as much as losing Steppin.

The last thought that would cross my mind would be of never again being able to stretch my arms towards the sun-lit sky, as Steppin and I used to do each time we swam under water.

My body would be found way downstream, far away from the place where Steppin had left me. When everyone saw me dead, I reckoned, they would all be sorry about the way they'd treated me, but Steppin would be the sorriest of all.

I didn't want to die. I wanted to think Steppin wouldn't care what I had done in that place. Nor what I felt about him now sitting next to him on the riverbank. He must have got used to me spying on him out of the corner of my eye and just ignored it, as he did when other people stared at him.

I stopped thinking bad thoughts and looked back at my fishing pole. I knew nothing else mattered as long as I was Steppin's friend and he was mine.

After the sixth fat fish was landed, we decided we'd caught enough to call it a good morning's fishing. We shared the catch equally, hanging it in the shade until we were ready to go home. Then, after putting our fishing poles high up on the grassy part of the riverbank, we turned to the serious business of doing nothing for the rest of the morning.

We lay back in the long dry grass and watched the bare stalks gently waving about our heads. The seeds, if they had ever developed in the baking drought, had long vanished. With the whole world seemingly draped in a blanket of sunshine,

Steppin and I chewed on a stalk of grass each and dozed, letting the heat and sweat from our bodies keep us languid. The shadow of the occasional white cloud drifted over us and away again, leaving a brief spot of coolness to soothe our skins.

"Mickey?" I heard Steppin ask through my closed eyes. I could tell it was a determined sort of question he was going to ask me.

"Yeah, Steppin," I replied, taking the stalk out of my mouth. Whatever he was going to ask, I wanted to be able to answer clearly.

"Your rules," he started to say, but stopped.

I knew that he was not sure whether to go on. He was unsure whether asking me more would cause me to go loony on him again like I had the last time.

"Wh.. what about them?" I knew he was going to ask things I didn't want to answer, but I tried not to lose my head. If I did, I might lose him that way, even if I didn't tell him anything.

I had told him I couldn't go into town and my Pa didn't want me to help him and I wasn't allowed to have any friends, but I'd never told him why. I was too scared to tell him any of that.

"Why did your Pa make them up for you?"

It was the one question I didn't want him to ask, but I'd always known he would. I couldn't say a thing. I felt my face go all red and my hands go all sticky with sweat. I tried to think about what to tell him and how I could tell him in a way that wouldn't drive him away from me.

I thought about lying, but if he found out the truth, that would make things even worse. I thought about saying nothing, but I couldn't. If he wanted to know, he'd find out one way or another. I had to tell him and take the enormous risk of losing him. It wasn't fair to him if he found out from other people.

I turned my head to face him, putting my right hand under my head for support. It took me a long time, but I told him what had happened, all the time watching him in case he started to look disgusted and want to run away from me. I'd stop then, if it wasn't too late.

But he didn't say or do anything. Once or twice he frowned a little, but maybe it was because of what someone else had done and not me. Then I thought maybe he knew it all anyway, putting it together from what I'd already told him or what his Ma and Pa had said.

His Ma and Pa had been here long enough to learn what everyone thought about me. I was stupid, troublesome, rude and had all sorts of nasty habits which they didn't want their children to pick up.

They must have heard I'd peed myself in the Principal's office. It wasn't my fault. He hadn't listened when I said I had to go to the bathroom real urgent. He was the one who told me to stay in his office, perfectly still, so I wouldn't get into more trouble. I proved him wrong. Even standing still I could be trouble.

Everyone knew that my teacher couldn't handle me. I couldn't help it if I didn't understand what she was going on about. She was always trying to get numbers into my head that didn't fit. It wasn't my fault if they went in one ear and out the other. She got mad when I asked questions when I didn't understand and she got mad when she asked me questions that I didn't understand.

That time she'd made me stand up in front of everyone and write the numbers on the board, the ones she'd just told me. I got all confused. Then she asked me to recite my times tables and I couldn't do that either. Even though they weren't making any noise, I could see all the children were laughing and that made things worse. I couldn't remember anything then.

The teacher said I should speak proper and stop trying to make a fool of her. I told her I wasn't trying to make a fool of her. The words didn't come right out the way I wanted. My mouth was the wrong shape.

That made all the kids laugh out loud. Then she got really mad. She hated it when the kids made a noise. She told me she would give me one last chance and asked me another question. I was so confused, I didn't know what to say. I wanted to say something, but all these words kept bubbling up in my head and none of them would come out.

Then I just kind of screamed at her. I wasn't really screaming at her but that's what she thought. I was just trying to get the words out, to get it all clear in my mind. Maybe I did say "bitch". It was the worst word I could think of, but I didn't really want to call her that. It just came out.

It wasn't the first time she had picked on me. She was really mean and I hated her. She used to make me show off my hands to the rest of the class to try and stop me biting my nails. I couldn't stop it. Half the time I didn't even know I was doing it. Then she'd get mad at me because I couldn't tell her who the President was. I could never remember.

When she asked questions like that I'd feel my neck go all hot and my face sweat. Once when I couldn't say anything, a kid had called out "Dumbo!" then all the other kids had joined in. "Dumbo! Dumbo!" She didn't stop them and I ran out of the class and all the way home. When my Pa found out, he tanned me and sent me straight back in.

I got sent to the Principal with a note. I tried to read it, but I couldn't understand it. The Principal read the note and made me stand in the corner while he went to speak to the teacher. When he came back, I'd peed all over his floor. Then he called my Pa and that was that. Well, it wasn't. There was more, but I didn't tell Steppin. What I'd said was bad enough.

I knew it wasn't my fault. I couldn't help being the way I was. I couldn't help being dumb, horrible and ugly and all the other stuff people called me. I couldn't help the fact I couldn't read or count or the way I talked. But everyone said it was my fault the way I behaved — all the other kids, my teacher, the Principal and my Ma and Pa.

That was why Pa had given me all these rules, until I behaved better. That was why I hated that place and never wanted to go back. They'd never want me back and I'd never want to go.

All the while I was telling him this, Steppin didn't say anything. He didn't laugh or turn up his nose when I told him how I'd peed my pants or any of the other stuff. He acted like he was sorry for me and none of what had happened was my fault.

While I was talking, I just kept watching Steppin. I never tired of looking at his face. There was nothing wrong with it. Not like me. He didn't have any moles and his ears didn't stick out and he didn't have any freckles. He was just the perfect kid, with perfect skin and perfect hair. Everything was perfect for him. His Ma and Pa even liked him. I wished my Ma and Pa would like me too, just once maybe.

He was so perfect, I wondered why he wanted to spend so much time with me. How come he wanted to just lie here, besides me of all people, on my muddy riverbank?

Sally Ives

Now that I'd started talking, I couldn't stop. I told Steppin more, even though I thought I shouldn't, cause then he'd really know what kind of boy I was. He wouldn't want to be with me any more. That's what had happened with all the other kids I knew, from the other farms around. As soon as they heard about what happened, they dropped me like a hot cake that had burnt their fingers. They didn't like me any more. I didn't blame them.

There was a girl called Sally Ives that I really hated. Nobody liked her and because she was bigger than me she picked on me all the time. Knowing no one would come to my rescue made her bully me even more. She was always laughing at how dumb I was and the way I spoke and she'd even begun to hit me. She knew I wouldn't hit her back because she was a girl and she knew I wouldn't tell on her because everyone would laugh at me being bullied by a girl.

That day there was just me and her in the classroom. She started calling me Dumbo and other names. I told her to leave me alone but the words wouldn't come out right and that made her even nastier. I tried to leave but she was standing in front of the door and wouldn't let me out.

Then she grabbed hold of my shirt so I couldn't get away. She was really enjoying herself, calling me a coward and a sissy. I knew she was right. There was nothing I could do to get away from her or make her stop. Then, before I knew what was happening, she'd pulled her right leg back and let me have it, right between my legs.

I staggered and swayed with the impact, but somehow managed to remain standing. Until the bomb she'd exploded between my legs reached my brain. Then my whole body tilted forward. I started to shake like a jelly and doubled up. As I went over onto my knees I heard myself cry a long, pitiful whine.

As I fell, I put my hands over the site of the explosion in my pants, and tried to squeeze the pain out from my balls. I didn't think I had them anymore. But I did. They were all on fire and I just gave myself more pain.

I sucked in several deep breaths but it didn't get any easier. It was like my whole body was in pain that just went on and on. I thought she'd hit me so hard that she'd killed me and I was dying from the pain.

I looked up, thinking she was going to hit me on the face and head like she usually did. But she just stood there watching as I gulped for breath and the tears streamed from my eyes. Then I thought she was going to kick me again and I kept my hands over my pants, imagining what they were going to feel like when her foot hit them.

I couldn't keep looking up. I waited for her to hit me again. It didn't matter where. But she didn't need to hit me. It was all over. She'd proved that I was nothing, no one, a zero kid. And I'd proved it too by not doing anything. I'd just let her hit me and now all I could do was lie there.

She waited until she'd had enough watching me dying in front of her. Then she said "Bye, Dumbo," and flounced off.

The pain was kind of different now, in my stomach as much as between my legs. I managed to get up and crawl over to the restroom. I was lucky there was no one there. I sat down and pulled down my pants to see what damage she had done. I was afraid to look, in case there was blood there. Maybe I didn't have anything left and then all the boys would really laugh at me.

Then suddenly I was sick all over the floor. After that I peed myself and that made the pain come back again. All the time I was groaning and moaning, but no one heard or came and helped me.

I didn't tell anyone what had happened. Even though it took me over an hour to walk home, every step agony. It was weeks till all the pain had gone.

But Sally Ives told. She told the other girls and they told all the boys and pretty soon everyone knew. They were all disgusted by what I had let happen to me. I wasn't a boy, just a coward. If I was a proper boy, I would have hit her after she started to bully me. You could hit a girl if she hit you first. Then they couldn't say you were picking on them. But I hadn't hit her at all. I'd just let her kick me in the worst possible place.

I knew I had punished myself again by telling Steppin. He wouldn't be my friend now. He'd be disgusted too. Or maybe he'd just laugh at me. Or he'd tell his parents and they'd tell him to keep away from me. I thought about what all the other kids would think if they knew what I had lost by telling the one person I wanted to keep my faults from. They would smile with glee. They would be really glad at what had happened to me.

When I'd finished, I turned away and stared at the flowing river, not wanting to see his face any longer, to see what he thought. I didn't want him to see mine either, cause I'd begun to cry. Now that he knew, I felt like I was drowning. I was afraid to look back round, cause I was sure he wasn't going to be there any more.

But at the same time it was a relief to let it out. I hadn't told anyone about it since it had happened. I had kept it all inside. Ma had asked and Pa had tried to make me tell him, but I hadn't said a word.

"It's lunchtime, I reckon," I heard Steppin say. "You'd better get the lemonade, Mickey," he added as he reached for our sandwiches.

I sniffed back my tears and stood up, turning to hide them as I wiped my right hand over my face and nose. Maybe everything was going to be all right.

"H.. hot, isn't it?" I said, wanting to say something to keep him here. I still didn't look at him, though, as I wiped my fingers on the rear pocket of my overalls then got rid of the last of the snot on the front of my thigh.

"Yep. Sure is."

I felt he was just saying something for my sake. If he had said nothing, I would have died on the spot.

So that Steppin wouldn't see I had been crying, I was very slow going to get the lemonade and took my time coming back. I saw, on the way back, that he had held out for as long as he reckoned reasonable before he bit into his sandwich.

I had kept my mind on the task of untying the strings that held the bottles. They were as cold as they always were. I made my way slowly back up the riverbank, trying not to think of what he would do now he knew all about me. I passed one of the bottles to Steppin as he held out a sandwich to me.

"Thanks," we both said at the same time. I laughed and smiled a little. He did too. I saw things weren't going to be that bad after all. He had smiled again.

I ate my sandwich and sipped on the cold lemonade, mostly in silence, shy of looking in his direction at all. He knew all about me now. More than most people did, in fact.

"I need a piss," I heard him say suddenly and I watched as he put his lemonade bottle down, got up and went off to stand against the bushes. Seeing him pissing and the look of sheer pleasure on his face as he sprayed the steady stream all around him made me jealous. He didn't seem to have a care in the world.

Watching Steppin piss and shake himself dry, I thought he was so lucky to be happy the way he was. I wished I was.

It was hot and still. All we could hear were our own voices, the sound of the river as it gurgled along and some wading birds chirruping as they dashed along the bank below us looking for something to eat in the mud.

I had destroyed the patch of mud immediately in front of us, searching for worms to tempt the fish with. I knew the birds would not find anything to eat there. I could have told them not to bother to look but they wouldn't take any notice of me. No one did.

"Were the sandwiches alright?" Steppin asked as he came back to lie down right next to me and join me staring at the sunny blue sky.

"Yeah, th.. they were great," I said.

"And the lemonade?"

"It was great too," I said, sitting up and resting on my elbows as I turned to look at him. "Your Ma's real good at making lemonade."

I looked at his green diamond eyes, not looking for their beauty, just some sign that told me he still liked me, or at least he didn't hate me.

He didn't look any different from before. He had the same smile on his face, not like the other children who hated me or ran away from me.

I'd heard somewhere that a problem shared was a problem halved. I began to think that maybe things weren't so bad after all.

"Want to go swimming in a while?" Steppin asked, as if nothing between us had changed.

"Sh.. sure I do," I said. We always had a swim after our lunch had gone down.

I didn't understand why Steppin wasn't running away or laughing at me, but I didn't care. To him the day wasn't any different from any of the others we had spent together, no matter what it seemed to me. Suddenly the whole world seemed different and not so bad after all.

Scare

I always enjoyed swimming in my river. It was the one thing that always made me feel better when I was down.

When we'd waited enough after lunch, I took off my overalls and dropped them next to my fishing pole. Then I thought better of it and flicked them over the battered but still precious pole, hiding it from anyone who wanted to steal it. Nobody walked by here, but I'd nearly lost my pole that way last summer when I was fishing nearer town. I wasn't going to risk losing it again.

Steppin was out of his boots and jeans and shirt as quickly as me, but he was more careful with his clothes. He folded them neatly, shirt on top of the jeans and both on top of his boots, while I usually threw mine down any old how.

I reckoned his Pa must have more money than mine, and probably could afford his son to come back home with dirty, scuffed clothes, but Steppin kept pretty much tidy anyway.

We bombed into the river, surfacing a dozen yards off the river bank.

"Race you to the other side," Steppin said. When we first met, I didn't think he could be a good swimmer. He looked so delicate, I didn't think he'd be allowed to learn. I thought his Ma and Pa would think he was too precious to let near the water. Though I suppose I had answered my own question. A kid as precious as Steppin would have been taught to swim just to keep him safe.

I set off after him. He would soon tire, I told myself. He did so soon, slowing to a steady stroke. I wanted to win this race, but held off until we reached halfway across and then edged in front. This spurred him on to try and catch up with me. I edged away again, tempting him by appearing to drop my pace. I laboured my breathing and appeared to give up, then shot ahead as he reached me, laughing inside at my own cleverness.

A few strokes further on, I looked back. He had been behind me. But he wasn't there any more.

"Steppin?" I called, but there was no answer. He was gone.

I looked ahead again, trying to see if he had beaten me. No, the bank was empty. I looked around and behind me again to see if he had given up and headed back to the other side.

He wasn't there.

I was really scared. It left only one thing. I took a deep breath and dove beneath the surface to look for him.

I had to find him. I just had to. Not only for Steppin's sake, but for mine. My Pa would skin me alive for disobeying the rules. Steppin's Pa would skin me alive for letting his son die. Everyone would blame me if Steppin drowned. They'd say I led him on. They might even say I'd pushed him down. They'd send me to the electric chair or maybe I'd spend all the rest of my life in jail.

The water was muddy and I could hardly see. I felt around but couldn't find him. I came back up again, desperately hoping to see him swimming along as if nothing was wrong. All I wanted was to see him alive. There was nothing.

Then I felt hands grab my ankles from below and pull. My mouth was still open as I disappeared under the water. I knew whose hands they were. I shut my mouth, pushing out the water that had already spilled inside. I looked down and I could just see through the water Steppin's pale back as he swam away.

As I struggled back up to the surface I was so glad to see he hadn't drowned, but I swore at him in my head at the same time.

You bastard! I thought, seeing Steppin laughing as he swam away from me, kicking his legs furiously. *You scared me rotten.*

I saw him dive under the water again, and set off after him to get revenge. I could see by the ripples on the surface where he was.

I was quicker than him and soon caught up with him. I reached down, grabbed his right ankle and yanked it, paying him back for scaring me to death. I swore under my breath as he kicked my hand with his other foot, forcing me to let go. His big toenail scratched my wrist.

Still under the surface, he swam off. This time I dove under to follow him, kicking my legs furiously to reach for him again.

He had to stop to breathe. Then I would get him. I had longer to go before I needed to surface again. I rushed at him under the water, to where he was treading water above me, breathing hard to recover from the effort needed to escape me.

I took my opportunity and pounced. As I grabbed him tight around the waist, I surfaced for a breath. That forced him even further out of the water before I dove again, pulling him down with me.

I held on tight to his waist as he wrestled to get free. I could see him smiling even though he was hitting my chest with the back of his elbows, and squirming furiously in my grip. I'd never held him in this way and it gave me that funny feeling again, even though we were under water and he was wriggling around the way he was.

As he struggled, his long hair swished backwards and forwards in slow motion in the water. It made him just as beautiful under the water as he was above it.

I was running out of breath when he managed to punch me on the nose with an elbow, making me let go of him and join him, struggling to the surface.

"B.. bastard!" I yelled as I surfaced, rubbing my bruised nose, pretending it was hurt much more than it was.

"Bastard!" he yelled back, holding his stomach under the surface where I'd caught him and held on.

I laughed, not wanting him to think that I had meant it. He laughed as well. I was so relieved. I didn't want to lose my friend.

We wrestled some more, above and beneath the water. We swam and raced and dove to pick up mud to throw at each other, then swam some more, trying to impress each other with our swimming skills.

I told Steppin that when the river was less muddy, I liked to chase the fish under the water, twisting and turning with them as they tried to get away. But they would always escape, being too quick for me. Once I got bored with that, I said, I'd race the ducks on the surface, chasing after them as they rushed away from me, flapping their wings and quacking furiously.

Sometimes, I told him, I just lay on my back in the river, like we were doing now, and drifted off downstream, watching the sky above as the river took me away from the farm. I would float further and further away. No one would see me, floating in the river like a leaf, arms outstretched, head just above the surface.

"That's neat," he said when I told him how I felt when I did that.

Watching Steppin as he floated beside me, like a brown autumn leaf, was great. He was happy. I was too. We swam up and floated down many times.

It seemed like hours before we beached up on the riverbank like two stranded whales, exhausted. We'd both had to struggle back upstream and so decided it was time to stop.

Climbing out of the water by our clothes and fishing poles, we slumped down on the grass. The clothes and fishing poles had, as usual, lain undisturbed.

As we dried in the sun, I sneaked another look at Steppin. He was looking up at the sky as I checked him out. His chest was pumping hard as he regained his breath.

His peter was bigger than mine. That didn't surprise me. Every boy had a bigger peter than I did. All I had was a cigar butt.

He didn't look as thin as when I had first seen him. Certainly he ate a lot. Every day there was his Ma's well-stuffed lunch bags and he probably had some real tasty cooking at night at home. I sometimes thought I could smell Steppin's supper on the breeze that drifted up from his place to ours. Then I wished I was Steppin tasting the delights of his Ma's cooking.

Even with the suncream he put on every day, his sun-tan was almost as deep as mine. Three weeks of going round with me, fishing, swimming, and dozing in the sun saw to that. I reckoned he probably hadn't gone skinny-dipping in the river where he had come from. Certainly not as much as we did together, nor fished so much either. He can't have had such a good time as he did with me, I thought, if there was no fishing or swimming.

He looked a lot happier now.

As he turned to look at me and his face caught the sun-light, I gulped and quickly looked away, not wanting him to catch me looking at him again. The longer I had looked at him, the more I had got that funny feeling again. I was thinking something about him too and I was scared in case he guessed what it was.

"What's wrong Mickey?" I heard him ask. He must have seen my face scrunch up when the thought I had been thinking for only a second got through my brain and onto my face.

"N.. nothing, Steppin," I said, sitting up a bit. That way he might not notice what was happening to my peter. I placed my right hand under my chin to support it and looked, but not in a staring kind of way, at his face.

He did the same, gently brushing his long wet hair off his forehead. Then he reached forward and shook my head. "Wh.. what're you doing?" I asked, as a pile of water that had been trapped in my black curls dribbled down my forehead onto my face.

"You need a towel Mickey, to dry that rug of yours," he said. "Your Ma'll want to keep you in to wash it tomor-row." My Ma always washed my hair every week.

"I suppose she will," I said, wiping the water off my face.

My hair was getting long. I loved it. I wanted it to be the same length as Steppin's. But I knew my Pa would soon hand me some money — not for a gift, but to get a haircut.

"You need a towel too, to dry that mop of yours," I said, swiping his hair forward and down over his eyes with a quick flick of my hand across his head. He shook it back with a flick of his head. I loved it. That movement took only a second and worked every time, clearing his face of his long hair. With a little help from his fingers, he stroked the remaining stray hairs behind his right ear.

"We could get a towel at m.. my house," I said, "b.. but my Pa wouldn't let me bring you in." Steppin could be soaking wet, shivering from the cold, even dying, and my Pa wouldn't let him inside our farmhouse, just because he was my friend.

"You could come in our house," Steppin said. "Mom would let you dry your hair in front of our range if it really needed it."

I gave Steppin his due. He was brilliant when it came to being sly. He thought that if I impressed on his folks how harmless I could be, they would tell my folks when they met them, "You've got a really nice kid there." Then my Pa would have to relent and let me bring Steppin into our house like I was a normal kid.

One day, maybe, a miracle would happen.

We pulled our clothes on quickly and ran back to Steppin's house. Luckily, my peter had gone all quiet again and Steppin didn't notice anything. Sitting in front of the range in his kitchen, our hair dried quickly.

Steppin's Ma had given us each a glass of milk and Steppin poured us both another one. It had come from their own cows that morning. Steppin's Pa had bought three. He wanted to buy a dozen, enough to sell the milk in town. It sounded like a good idea, but I never did understand business. It was good milk and that was all I cared about.

As I saw Steppin fill our glasses with even more milk, I reckoned to myself I would soon be swimming in it. My stomach was full and my bladder was already beginning to protest. I'd be peeing pure milk all the way back to my place.

When our hair was dry, it was too late to go back to the river. I said to Steppin and his Ma that I'd better be heading on home. I thanked his Ma politely for the milk and being able to dry my hair in front of her range. Both Steppin and I knew I was trying to impress her so she'd have to invite me back again. I looked at her right in the eyes. She had long fair hair, but not as light as Steppin's, and a real nice smile, just like his.

She bit my hook and I reeled her in as she smiled back. "That's alright, Mickey, it was a pleasure."

When I wanted to be, I could be cute and all that stuff parents wanted their kids to be. When I wanted to be, that is. I could see Steppin behind her watching us. He was holding the delicate fingers of his right hand over his mouth, imitating gagging sounds.

"See your guest to the door, Steppin," his mother said.

He stood up and came over to the door. "See you to-morrow?" he asked out on the porch.

"Sh.. sure thing, Steppin," I said, walking off and waving to him. All the way home I tried to imitate his bouncy walk. One day I'd be able to do it just right.

6

Harvest

Who's that?" Steppin asked the next day when we were out walking. "Mr Wilkins." He was a neighbor of ours I'd always liked until I got into trouble. "That his land?"

I nodded. We were spying on him from a distance as he sat on the top of his combine harvester, reaping the first of the summer's already bountiful harvest. I sure liked that word.

"You want to go ask if we can help?" Steppin asked. "I should get in some practise for when I've got to help around the farm. Pa says it's too dangerous to help plough or sow. But harvest time he says he'll let me help if I'm careful."

He brushed his sun-bleached fringe off his face and waited for my reply. He would have to have his hair cut soon. Even more of it was falling in his eyes. If he'd let me, I thought, I'd cut his fringe for him. I was good with knives and could handle scissors well. If he let me cut it, I could keep a lock of it in my secret box.

"Okay," I said, answering his question before my brain could think. "We'll have to hurry." The combine was moving away from us.

Or maybe, I thought, I could sneak a piece of Steppin's hair from off the barber's floor, if he got his hair cut in town. Unless of course his Ma cut it for him.

Steppin was halfway across the fence that surrounded the Wilkins farm before I realized what he was doing.

"S.. Steppin, I can't," I said.

"How come? Oh, your..." He climbed down from the fence.

"Yeah, m.. my rules." Watching Steppin climb over the fence had made me remember them. Pa wouldn't let me off the farm to help Mr Wilkins or anyone else for that matter. Even if I didn't tell Pa, Mr Wilkins would be bound to tell him.

We watched Mr Wilkins in the distance, on his combine moving even further away.

I saw the machine throwing out piles of straw that waited to be collected by his son, who was pulling a baler behind the other tractor.

"I could ask to help," Steppin said as a flash of inspiration hit him. He looked at me, a big smile on his face.

What?

I looked at Steppin right in the face, shrugging my shoulders and feeling them slump right down. "Sh.. sure," I said, "if you want." I couldn't stop him. I was the only one who couldn't help Mr Wilkins. Steppin had no rules to stop him from helping anyone or going anywhere he wanted!

"I'd better be getting home then," I said, turning away from him and the Wilkins farm to start the longest trudge of my life. I would go to my river and cry my eyes out, or kill myself.

I might even do both, I thought.

Steppin had dumped me for the chance to work on Mr Wilkins' farm! My Mr Wilkins, not his! Some friend he turned out to be. He was just like the rest.

"No, Mickey," he said, pulling me back and turning me around. "You can't help him, but you can help me helping him, can't you? That's not against your rules, is it?"

It still meant going off the farm, but I'd been going over to Steppin's place every day and my Pa hadn't said anything. On Mr Wilkins' land I'd still be with Steppin, so it wasn't very different. Maybe if I asked nicely, Mr Wilkins wouldn't say anything to my Pa. They weren't real close neighbors. But then Mr Wilkins had a real good reason not to like me.

It all worked out. Steppin hadn't forgotten. He just had brains. I felt really happy again.

Mr Wilkins looked at me without saying anything while Steppin explained what we wanted to do. He even promised not to tell my Pa as long as we didn't get in the way. That was real good of him, considering what he knew about me. Soon Steppin and I were both sweating hard as we lifted bale after bale of dusty straw onto the trailer bed that John, Mr Wilkins' son, had brought up after finishing the baling.

Mr Wilkins, to my relief, was soon off back to the farm, leaving his son to finish off while he attended to the growing stack in the barn. John seemed as strong as three ordinary men. He could have done all the baling and stacking by himself but he didn't seem to mind having Steppin and me around to help.

No matter how quickly we dragged a single bale to the trailer, John's broad muscles had already fetched two or three. But he would stop and heave ours up on top of the growing mountain, smiling and thanking us, as if ours was the most important one.

"Doing well, boys," he said.

We both looked up from where we were dragging another heavy bale towards him, feeling hot and sweaty as the sun beat down on us. He saw the look on our faces as soon as he had called us boys. We looked mad as hell, and were ready to explode with anger. We were only pretending, but he knew that calling us boys while we were doing a man's job in the fields wasn't right.

"Doing well... men!" he said.

We relaxed and smiled at him, and continued to heave the bale up onto one end, offering it to him. He took it, pulling on the two strings binding the straw together, lifted it and swung the bale above our heads so that it landed on top of the rest.

He then climbed onto the trailer and carefully arranged it amongst the others.

After I reckoned what must have been a couple of hours, Steppin and I dramatically wiped the sweat off our brows and shook the water off our arms and hands.

John took the hint.

"Lunch," he said, holding out his two strong hands so we could grasp one each with both of ours.

We held on tight as he lifted us up to a height which seemed a hundred feet above the ground, before swinging us over the tractor bed. His arms were fully outstretched, like a building crane. He set us both down gently.

I decided that I liked John Wilkins very much. He was strong, had a big hairy chest and lots of impressive muscles on his back and arms. All of them were dripping sweat in the burning sun. He was also friendly and kind, and treated us like he knew how young friends should be treated.

Steppin and I ate our lunches on the very top of the highest straw bales, despite John's fears that we might topple off.

"We'll be all right," Steppin said. "Besides, you'd catch us if we fell, you being so strong."

"Don't be so sure about that, young fellow," John said as he jumped off the trailer, preferring to eat his lunch on the ground.

After our sandwiches and apple pie, we had a swig of John's beer. After all, we told him, if we were doing real men's work we should be able drink real men's drink.

"Okay, okay, if it'll keep you quiet," John said, passing up the bottle. "Just don't let on, mind."

We shook our heads, crossed our hearts and said, "Never!"

He took the bottle back and settled back down to his own lunch.

John knows kids pretty well then, I thought. He wasn't that old himself and had a brother about our age, so he knew what kids liked. I bet he drank lots of beer when he was our age, I thought. I liked John Wilkins.

The beer was very different to our lemonade. It made my head go light. Which was the only reason, I told myself later, why I put my hand in Steppin's as we lay on top of the world, relaxing after lunch. Steppin didn't say anything or move his hand. He just let mine lie there.

We were too high up for John to see us. He was nice and kind to us kids but he was almost a grownup. Maybe he would understand what I felt about Steppin, I thought. But then again, maybe he wouldn't.

In the hot midday sun, the only thing that moved was a light breeze which appeared out of nowhere. It ruffled through the bales where we lay outstretched soaking up the rays, our eyes closed to the glare. We didn't care where it went. We were only glad that it cooled our skin. We closed our eyes and dozed in the heat.

"Come on you two, there's work to be done," I heard John's quiet voice suddenly above me. He had climbed up the bales so quietly carefully that we hadn't heard or felt a thing.

I didn't like that. He could have just called us. As I opened my eyes and saw John, I snatched my hand out of Steppin's. I got up and scrambled down the mountain of straw, hoping that he hadn't really seen us holding hands. I didn't know what he'd do if he had.

"I've got to get back to the farm with this load," he said. "Pa needs me this afternoon. The rest of the bales will have to wait till tomorrow."

"Can we help then?" Steppin asked, before I even thought that it would be nice to help John finish off the field we had all worked in together.

"Sure, if you really want."

Stupid question, but we forgave him. I also forgave him for being sneaky. He had woken us up nicely and not shouted as some people would.

"Yes, sir!" we said together, nodding our heads at the same time.

He drove off and we walked back to the edge of the field. I felt Steppin trying to hold my hand. I didn't dare let him, in case John looked back and saw. He might tell his Pa.

Only when we were over the fence and on the way to the river did I think it was safe to hold Steppin's hand again. Neither of us said anything about it, but it sure felt good.

Lazy Afternoon

Down by the river we decided to go for our usual swim. Steppin was in the water first and splashing about as I took off my overalls and ran down the bank and bombed into the river just near him.

"Dipstick!" I heard him cry as I disappeared under the water. I closed my eyes as soon as I saw the silt on the river bottom well up in response to the underwater wave I'd created.

Surfacing, I saw Steppin shake his head, its wet curtain of hair swishing about, shedding the water my splash had deluged him with.

I laughed and skipped my arm across the surface of the water, splashing a wave of water in his direction. He closed his eyes and took the full force of the wave in his face.

When he opened them, I saw revenge in his green eyes. I yelped and dove out of the way of whatever he had planned, pushing off the bottom of the river bed to start swimming away from him as fast as I could.

"No, no, no," I cried as he caught up with me. I took a deep breath as he dunked me under the water.

I didn't struggle too hard to try and get free of his tight grip as he pulled me down with him. It was his revenge, and exactly the same thing I'd done to him many times. I was strong, but I let him bounce me off the bottom of the river.

We broke the surface together.

Seeing him swimming just yards from me, I was so glad that he was with me. What I had told him the other day about me hadn't stopped him being my friend.

I wanted to hug him but didn't dare. I just smiled at him, glad that everything was alright between us.

I was rewarded with a beaming smile right across his clear face, punctured once again with bright green emeralds, crystal clear as the water in which we swam.

It seemed to both of us, I thought, that the many hours we spent together in the river swimming, racing across its width, seeing who could make it without surfacing for a breath, were the best hours and days ever spent by two boys free to do what they wanted with water without having to wash in it.

After an hour or more we both decided we'd had enough of swimming and we swam to the edge. Finding my feet on the river bed, I stood up and got out, intent on climbing to the top of the riverbank, to lie down under the sun once more.

"It's too hot up there," Steppin said as he clambered out of the water. "I'm going to stay here."

Sitting down in the river mud just above the water line, Steppin rested his feet and legs in the water and lay back, making sure his long hair was out of the mud and against a mound of grass.

"You're right," I said, copying his weary attitude and sitting down next to him, splashing and wriggling into the mud. I leant back and covered my eyes with the crook of my left arm. I knew Steppin would also adopt the same stance. Shielded from the sun in that way, we set about the serious business of dozing.

Lying there, as the afternoon wore on, I found the courage to take a chance and do something I had wanted to for many days, weeks even — probably ever since I first met Steppin.

I lifted the crook of my left arm off my face, but, still shielding my eyes, turned to check that Steppin's eyes were shut tight against the sun and from the glare coming off the water. Then I moved my right arm from across my belly, and placed it carefully next to Steppin's head.

I covered my eyes again with my left arm before I let the fingers of my right hand gently touch Steppin's hair. After a moment, when I felt no shaking of my hand off his head, I took my arm slowly away from my eyes and looked to see my hand still there, resting on his fine, shiny, sun-bleached mop. Steppin didn't move or look at me. His eyes were closed, like he was asleep.

I almost couldn't believe what I saw and felt, but it was real. His hair felt so nice under my hand. I wanted to move it down to touch his forehead but didn't dare.

Tears welled up inside me and spilled over my eyes, running freely down my cheeks. I bit my lips and kept my mouth closed to stop the sobs already building up within me. As I breathed slowly in and out, trying to cry quietly so he wouldn't hear me, my chest trembled with the tears.

I didn't know why I felt so bad, yet so happy all at the same time, touching his hair and wanting to touch his face. What was it that made me feel the way I did about him?

The sun was still shining as bright as it had been every day Steppin and I came to the river, our river. I thought it should have exploded, just like my heart felt like doing, burning my badness away.

Steppin, I knew, was all that I was not and could never be — attractive, good and loveable.

As I lay there, my brain worked at a speed of about a million miles an hour, thinking of so many things all at once. I knew summer was going to end sooner or later. There were only a few days before Steppin started the daily bus trip to that place, as he started his education once again. Then I'd be alone every day.

I had to do something to keep him. But whatever I did might very well drive him away from me. It was a terrible risk, but if I didn't do something, I knew that one day he would look up, and turn away from just wanting me for his only friend.

I wanted him to be my friend, mine and mine alone. I didn't want to share him with anyone, no matter who.

I could carry his books every morning to the bus for him, I thought, and hand them to him just before he got on. And I could meet him every day when he came back and he could tell me everything that had happened at that place. But then the other kids would see me, and laugh at me and turn him against me, tell him all about me, and what I had done to them. I'd been too frightened to tell him everything.

In my darkest nightmares, I saw that he would find someone else to be his friend. He would meet lots of boys every day. There was bound to be someone he liked better than me. Then he would go off and leave me alone again.

I tried to think of the time before he entered my life. It was frightening and empty. I hated being alone. I let go of another batch of tears when I thought of the gaping hole that would be left in my life if he left me now.

I thought the only way I could keep him was if I went to that place with him. But I couldn't. Nothing, not even Steppin, could make me go back there again.

I was going to lose Steppin, I knew. Summer and all my happiness were going to come to an end.

Forever Friends

Steppin didn't notice me crying. In a while my tears stopped and I began to feel a little better. I thought that whatever was going to happen, lying here together in the squishy mud of the river like pigs in a wallow was just great. We were safe from any prying, jealous eyes as we basked in the glorious sunlight that marked our friendship.

I took my hand off his head, away from his beautiful hair, and leaned up on my elbow in the mud. I wanted to look at his face as I had done so many times. I suppose I could have made a living as a Peeping Tom, the amount of time I spent looking at Steppin.

I moved my legs about a little in the cool water, enjoying the feeling against the hairs that had just began to grow.

It was nice to be able to be messy, especially with mud, without being told off. I thought that everyone should have a nice squishy piece of mud to lie in every now and again. It was even better with a friend to share it with.

"S.. Steppin..." I started to say, wanting to tell him something that I knew I just couldn't keep inside me any longer.

No one else would understand. Steppin, I hoped, would.

Knowing something is wrong doesn't stop people doing it, I told myself. Look at all the killing that went on in Korea.

While I waited for him to open his eyes and sit up, I thought that the river now really belonged to both of us. It was a nice idea after all, sharing the river. Especially with Steppin.

That wasn't the thought I wanted to share with him though.

He opened his eyelids to reveal his green emeralds. They were bright and wide, as always. As he leaned up on his elbows, then sat himself up right next to me, I was glad he was my friend.

I also knew that I should have stopped myself right then.

He didn't stop me when I put my right arm around his muddy shoulder. I knew that boys did that to their girls when they were getting all romantic and slushy. Me doing it to Steppin wasn't the same. I felt his left arm around my shoulder as he copied me.

I think he could see my eyes were wet again.

Then I started to shake, like I shook the other time when I went off my head. As I did, I reckoned that Steppin thought I was going loony again, because he put his other arm around me and held me tight.

As he held me, I told him that I didn't need anyone any more, not for anything. It was true. Apart from him, that is.

I felt him nod, but he didn't say anything. His long hair bobbed over my head.

He listened to me telling him that I didn't need any friends. I had got loads of enemies, especially after what happened.

I didn't tell him that bit, though. What I'd done had frightened them all, I remembered. It had scared them to death. I was glad I'd done it, too. It showed them all that I hated them, and that I was prepared to do what I said I would.

They had learned what it felt like to be afraid, just as I was, not sure whether I'd be able to get home without a bloody nose, or without my balls feeling like they had been kicked into a pulp.

I knew that blood could be wiped off and bruises faded but what was left was the pain inside and all the questions. My pain was invisible to them and I pretended that they couldn't hurt me, no matter what they did. But though they couldn't see it, it was like an open sore, never comforted, never fading, just sitting there, oozing and seeping pain.

I asked Steppin the same question I wanted to ask them.

Why? Why pick on me? Why did they all want to hit me now? Why didn't they leave me alone if they didn't like me? And why wouldn't they ask me to join in with their games so we could become friends again? That was all I wanted and waited for, to be asked.

"They n.. never did," I said. "I hate them all!"

"Forget about them," Steppin said.

"I do, m.. most of the time" I said. "That's why I like being alone. Apart from b.. being with you, that is," I added quickly. "When I'm alone, there's n.. no one around to call me dumb, even in a f.. friendly kind of way. They said they w.. wanted to be f.. friends, and that I could j.. join in. But they hit me and s.. said it was part of the game. I hated them. I only w.. wanted to be f.. friends, but they d.. didn't!"

"I want to be your friend, Mickey." He let go of me a little, because he could see I wasn't going to lose my head after all.

"You are my friend, S.. Steppin. You're my best friend ever, even if I'm ugly and d.. dumb and stupid and a coward too!"

"I don't think you're any of these things," Steppin said, putting his hand over my mouth to stop me going on and on about how bad I was. "You're just great, really you are. You've got nice brown eyes and great curly hair," he said, tussling my head. "I like you, Mickey."

That made me feel so good I pulled him to me and hugged him tightly. "You're my best friend ever, in the entire world," I told him. He was, too. He was so honest about what he just said, I just had to believe he meant it. It wasn't a lie, like adults saying something to you that they didn't really mean.

I never thought anyone would ever say that to me, that they liked me with all my faults.

Steppin couldn't tell a lie even if he wanted to, not to me anyway. I could lie, and often did. But I knew if I heard just one forming on his thin red lips I would know right away what it was.

I told Steppin again that I hated all the other kids. Even before my Pa gave me my rules, I hated every one of them as I watched them walk down the sidewalk in twos and threes or waiting for the bus to take them home from that place. They were always chatting like chipmunks and messing about as they walked ahead of me. No one was ever quiet apart from me. They should be quiet, I always thought, just like me.

I always walked to the bus on my own, behind all the other kids. Then I could watch the boys joshing with each each other, just like the girls did.

The girls always talked about the boys or their new dresses or whose house they were going to sleep over at next weekend. The boys talked about football or going out on their bikes with their friends when they got home.

No one noticed me on my own at the back. No one ever invited me to join them. Even when there were spare kids around, trailing behind me or to the side, no one ever talked to me or sat next to me on the bus unless they had to. They would rather stand than sit next to me, and that wasn't allowed.

I pretended I didn't care, and just stared out the window trying not to be noticed.

I told Steppin I didn't need any of that. I liked being alone, all alone. Alone meant that you didn't have to rely on anyone for anything. Alone meant that you never had to wait outside their houses for them, or in their kitchen, while they got their old boots on, or rushed about changing their pants, getting into ones they could mess up. Alone meant that you never giggled outside their open kitchen doors, waiting for them as their mothers insisted on their washing their faces and hands before they went out to play.

Being alone meant you could do things by yourself, like fishing or swimming or watching the birds and animals, or just walking. Being alone was great.

I tried to believe it myself.

"I like being with you, Mickey," Steppin said to me again. "You're great, you are."

"Thanks," I said, hugging him tightly again. I had hugged him more than I remembered ever hugging my Ma or Pa.

Before Steppin came to my river, I had felt so empty deep down, right inside me. I didn't let anyone know about it, no matter how bad it hurt. It was just like if I saw something I wanted but couldn't have, something then began squeezing me high up in my chest. It squeezed so hard that I felt as if I was dying for the lack of whatever it was that caused the feeling inside me.

It was like an illness that I didn't know the name of, so I called it my Black Emptiness. Whenever I felt bad, or rotten, or sad about my troubles, I felt my Black Emptiness.

I told him Steppin what my Black Emptiness was like. "It s.. squeezes me so hard that it hurts, as b.. bad as when S.. Sally Ives kicked me. The B.. Black Emptiness just keeps coming b.. back," I told him. "It doesn't ever go away. It's like a b.. bomb exploding inside my head. I feel like it's going to be there f.. forever. It's n.. never going to go away, Steppin!"

I couldn't stop telling him how I felt. "No one likes me, not even my Ma and Pa! They don't care about me. Everyone hates me! No one cares what happens to me!"

I was beginning to sob and shake again and Steppin held me close.

"I care about you Mickey," Steppin said. "I like you and care about what happens to you. Really I do."

"You do?" I asked. He'd said it before but I still couldn't believe it.

"Yes, I do." He was whispering, because his mouth was real close to my ear. I liked the feeling of his warm breath on my face.

"Thanks," I said, squeezing him some more.

"That's alright, Mickey, any time," he said.

Steppin held on to me, like he thought I might still go loony. I thought I certainly would have gone loony if he hadn't been holding me, thinking of all the things I was thinking about. But with Steppin there, I wasn't going to shout and scream. He made everything all right.

He knew I wasn't making things up or telling tales, like my Ma and Pa did when I used to tell them about the other kids at that place. He knew I felt as bad as I did. He just listened to me and said he was my friend. He was much better than my Ma and Pa or any friend had ever been to me.

Three Words

Neither of us said anything for a bit. I realized I had both my arms around him. One over his shoulder and one around his chest. He was holding me in the same way. I pulled back my head and looked into his eyes, watching as he blinked his eyelids. As he opened them, so gracefully, I felt rotten, because I was thinking one of my bad thoughts again.

"You all right?" he asked me, because I'd trembled a little.

I nodded and saw that his eyes were sparkling in the sunlight reflected off the water. I thought that they were even more beautiful like that, as was he.

"Sure?" he asked, checking again.

I nodded again, but didn't speak. He was my best friend. He was my only friend in the world. I felt so much I couldn't open my mouth to tell him how happy I was that he was there with me.

I could feel my heart beating harder and harder as more and more bad thoughts began swilling about in my head.

I shifted position slightly so that I was sitting beside him and we were both looking out over the river. I leant towards him like that, so that the side of his head touched mine. He didn't move. We stayed for a moment like that, side by side, watching the river move over our feet, before I pulled my head upright to turn to face him again. I waited for him to do the same. I still couldn't believe that he was my friend.

There was something I wanted to tell him, but I was afraid to open my mouth. I watched his eyes and his nose and his thin red lips as he waited for me to say whatever it was I wanted to say. I hesitated some more, but knew I just had to go ahead and tell him.

I was too scared to say the three words out loud, so I just whispered them.

I watched as the words sank into him. I was more scared of what he would say than I had ever been in my life.

I couldn't run away and hide, not while he held me. I couldn't take the words back or pretend they meant something else. They were plain enough for the dumbest person to understand.

He didn't say anything. I didn't know what he was thinking.

I thought maybe he didn't believe me. Maybe he thought I didn't know what I was saying So I had to prove it to him. I had to make him believe me. I leant towards him, and as softly and gently as I could think, kissed him on his left cheek.

Touching him like that, feeling his smooth, baby-soft skin beneath my thick, ugly lips, did something to me. It was hard to describe. It made me feel all warm, and flipped my stomach over into a tangle.

Only then did I realize what I had done. I tried to pull away from him, frightened.

I shouldn't have done it. But there was a fire burning in my chest so strong, that if I hadn't done something, if I hadn't shown him what I felt, I knew my heart would have exploded.

I had told myself I was just going to thank him for being my friend, for playing with me every day. And for saying that that he liked me, which was what I needed most. But there were all sorts of other things I wanted to tell him, things I wasn't sure I should say, like the fact he was beautiful and how he made me feel. It all got mixed up in my mind and instead of saying thank you, I ended up saying what I did and giving him a kiss.

Without thinking, I said the three words again and leant forward, closed my eyes and kissed him right on the lips, just like a boy would kiss a girl.

I couldn't help it. There was something inside me telling me it was alright to kiss him like that. He was my best friend.

Then suddenly, like I'd been turned upside down, I thought I'd done the worst ever thing I could do to him. More than that, I'd done it twice. He must hate me now. He'd never speak to me again.

I thought I was going to burst into tears at how unhappy I was, but I didn't have time. Steppin was too quick for me. He leant forward and kissed me on my lips, longer than I'd kissed him. His lips felt so warm as they touched mine I didn't want him to take them away. But he did.

Then I really did start to cry. I leant my forehead on his bare shoulder and heard myself sobbing like a baby. He leaned his head against mine as I continued to cry my eyes out. I felt his ear slide past mine, then felt the thin fingers of his right hand running slowly through my long, ugly, black curls. He began rocking me from side to side and making shushing noises. "It's alright, Mickey," he said. "Don't cry, it's all right."

But it wasn't all right. It was all wrong. What I, what both of us, had done was all wrong.

Boys were supposed to like girls. Boys couldn't kiss other boys. Boys couldn't think about other boys the way I thought about Steppin, all the things I didn't dare tell him. Maybe Steppin had just kissed me because he liked me, not because he felt about me the way I felt about him. What I wanted to do was wrong. It was the Devil's work.

At the same I was thinking these thoughts, I was thinking that Steppin was my friend, my only friend. I was hoping he wasn't mad at me for what I'd said and done. I was even hoping, even though I knew it was wrong, that he felt the same way about me. But then I thought I was wrong to think like that, because that meant I wanted him to be evil too, like me.

It was all wrong, me liking Steppin like he was a girl, even though I knew he wasn't a girl. I couldn't do with him all the things older boys did with girls. I couldn't hold his hand in case other people saw, like I was sure John Wilkins had done. I couldn't kiss him, like I saw boys kiss girls.

There were names for boys who liked other boys. I didn't want to be one. I couldn't let other people think Steppin was one.

I stopped crying, because I had no more tears left, and just stayed there, with my head on Steppin's shoulder and his arms around me.

"It's all right," he said again. "It's all right."

I kept holding him. I never wanted to leave him again, ever, but I knew that was impossible.

Then I thought how bad Steppin must be feeling after what I'd said and done to him. I thought of a way to make everything all right again, so that no one would know what had happened and I would never bother Steppin again.

I could leave him here on our riverbank and jump into the river and drown myself. I reckoned it would be better than people finding out what I felt or what Steppin and I had done. Steppin could say it was an accident, me killing myself. Then he would be all right and free from any evil, because it would have died with me.

I didn't tell him what I was thinking. I began to think maybe there were other ways. Maybe I could just stop liking him the way that I did. And even if I did like him that way, I didn't have to do anything about it. I could just be his friend, his best friend. And if I was lucky, he'd still be my best friend.

I took my chin off his shoulder and sat back to look at him, the tears still wet on my cheeks. He didn't look mad or anything like that, just the way he always looked. I couldn't stop myself. I reached over and kissed him again on the lips. Then I pulled back because my nose was running, like it always did when I cried.

I sat back and reached across for my overalls and got my handkerchief from the big front pocket. I wiped my face and offered it to him, but he didn't want it.

I didn't know what I felt. I felt both happy and sad. Happy because Steppin wasn't mad at me. After all I'd said and done he was still here sitting on the riverbank with me. But I was feeling sad because everything I felt about Steppin was wrong.

Then another feeling came to me. I looked at him sitting there, naked like I was after our swim. He was just too good, too beautiful. It was all his fault that I felt the way I did about him. I got really angry with him and before I knew it was telling him.

"Why d.. did you move here? Why did you come down to m.. my river? Why couldn't you j.. just leave me alone? You sh.. shouldn't have s.. spoken to me! You knew I wasn't allowed to s.. speak to n.. no one! You're j.. just too... too..."

He sat there, listening to me. He must have thought I'd gone crazy and there was nothing he could say or do to stop me.

"It's all your fault!" I went on. "You m.. made me like you. You sh.. should never have come to the old Parker place. You... you..."

I wanted to chase him away, as I should have chased him away from my river, the first day I had seen him, weeks ago. I wanted to hurt him so bad that he would never speak to me again. Then he would be just like the rest and I would be alone again just as I used to be.

To make him go away I hit him hard, the way I had hit those other kids. I bloodied his nose and pushed him away and kicked him in the same place and just as hard as Sally Ives had kicked me. But it didn't hurt him. He just sat there, watching me.

Then I realized that all my shouting and screaming and kicking were only in my head. It was what I thought about saying to him. In fact, I hadn't said anything at all.

"I'm s.. sorry, Steppin. I'm sorry," I said.

"What for?" Steppin asked.

"N.. othin'. Everythin'. No, nothin'," I said.

I was so happy that he was still there and I hadn't hurt him after all that nothing else that had happened that afternoon seemed important. Or maybe it was important, but somehow, I could work it out.

Time passed. "It's getting late, Mickey," Steppin said, looking up at the afternoon sun. It was going down fast. Turning to look for myself, I saw that he was right. Sitting up from where we had lain back down after we had dried our tears, I realized time had flown.

We had lain on our riverbank, motionless, holding each other's hands, not saying anything. There was not much else to say after what I had said and done to him.

"We'd better get back," I said.

"Yeah, we'd better," he agreed.

I got up, letting go of his hand. I had held it since what happened earlier. We went to wash the mud off our backs and legs in the river. I put my overalls back on. I waited while he washed the mud off and got dressed.

Climbing up the bank, heading toward the trail up to the dirt road, I looked at him as I put my right hand out, and saw him smile he put his against mine. We closed our fingers.

Was this so wrong, to like Steppin so much I'd want to hold his hand and then kiss him? I burned inside with guilt and evil, so hot that I was sure he could feel it through my fingers. I didn't let go, though.

I was holding the fishing poles and the bait can in my other hand. He had the trowel and the empty lunch bags. We said nothing to each other as we walked, the orange color of the setting sun behind us, lighting up our deeply tanned backs as it pointed the way back to our homes.

I left the ring of flowers he had made around my neck as we walked. He told me I was as nice as they were. He had made them with his delicate fingers, which I liked too.

I knew flowers were sissy things, but I didn't take them off. I wore them for him. I don't think he realized it was sissy for boys to give other boys flowers.

And I knew what I had told him was true.

7

Dreams

At night I couldn't sleep. I ran though all that had happened during the day in my mind. I went over and over the moment I had kissed him. I still couldn't believe that he had kissed me back. He had done that. He had actually kissed my thick, ugly lips.

Why?

I was so restless, not only thinking about what happened but also with the heat. It was as hot as it had been all day. I knew it would stay like that until past midnight, when the summer heat finally dissipated into the cloudless sky.

I knew that while I was with Steppin there was new life in my daily existence. Without him I had nothing.

I had expected him to push me away, smear my kiss from his lips and leave. I was so glad he didn't.

I knew there would probably be a misty dawn to greet the next day. It would be such a special day if there was. I really hoped the mist would come.

I lay there going through the memories of what I regarded as the most important day of my life like a cartoon flicker-book. While turning the pages over and over again, I heard the creaking and popping of wooden timbers inside and outside the house as they cooled from the heat of the day.

As I stared at the darkness in my room, I could see Steppin's face and read his smile, remembering the moment we had kissed.

I didn't care about the many tears I had shed. He had kissed me back, that was the important part.

Turning over onto my right side, a beaming smile forced itself onto my face. I reached over and put the hand that had held his under the corner of my pillow, keeping it as warm as it had been in his when we walked home.

Looking across from my pillow over to the far wall, I watched the shadows of the tall wide tree that grew outside my window as its moonlit branches reached inside my room.

As I looked, the thinnest branches, twigs almost, seemed to be silently flicking backward and forward, like thin painful canes beating against a thousand backsides leaning over a thousand desks, receiving just punishment.

I shuddered and turned over, pulling my sheet over my head, hiding from the punishment I knew was there for me and my wickedness.

I could feel the pain from the canes as my stomach churned. It seemed to be happening again, like it had happened so many times before.

They had tried that on me after the stern words and looks hadn't worked. The kids all laughed when I hobbled back to class clutching my backside, my face scrunched up in pain, trying not to cry. If I did, it would let them know they had won again.

I woke up to find I was shivering.

Even though I knew it was only a bad dream, I took my time in pulling the sheet off my head. Sheepishly, I turned and looked to the far wall, searching for the shadow canes, ready at an instant to pull the sheet back over my head to hide again.

They were gone.

The moon had risen over the house and no longer cast the shadow of the tree and its branches against the bedroom wall. It must be early in the morning, I reckoned. It was quiet and peaceful outside. The sun hadn't yet risen to start the dawn chorus.

My right hand was lost in the crumpled sheet which I had somehow managed to wrap round me like a cocoon just before the butterfly comes out.

It was covering my naked butt, protecting it from the shadow canes that I had gone to sleep dreaming about, all of which were seemingly aiming for me alone.

I unravelled myself from the bedsheet, covered in goosebumps and shivering freely from the cold that had invaded my room. I was taking no chances, so remained in a sitting position as I slid to the end of the bed. Once there, I pulled at the blankets I had earlier turned down and folded out of the way.

Pulling them up to my neck, turning the cotton bedsheet back over the top blanket, I slid down inside the bedclothes, tucking them under my chin. I could have gotten out of bed to close the window, but didn't like the idea of the walk across the cold boards.

I snuggled further down, already feeling that the goosebumps were beginning to go.

It was good to sleep in my own bed. Some nights I slept in the barn, which was where my Pa said I had to sleep if I didn't have a shower before going to bed.

I must admit I was still a bit muddy when I got home. I surprised Pa by having a shower. I knew he expected me to complain and stomp about before rushing out of the house to sleep in the straw, but I didn't.

Most nights I didn't mind sleeping in the barn, dreaming about this and that, just covered by straw and an old blanket I kept out there. But tonight I wanted to sleep between fresh smelling, clean, sheets.

I couldn't tell Pa why he got me to do what he wanted without him saying a word. I just enjoyed the dumbfounded look on his face. With the knowledge in my head that I would be seeing Steppin again in a very few hours, I shut my eyes again and went back to sleep.

I was too tired to have any more thoughts, which were good thoughts for a wicked boy like me to have, or bad thoughts for a good boy like Steppin. I was afraid that even thinking about them, the rest of the world would find out and there was no way the rest of the world would understand.

Morning

I was up in time to see my Pa go out of the door to tend the irrigation pump which he had used to great effect on our fields. He even let Steppin's Pa have the use of it every day.

Together they would haul it further down the riverbank and put its pipe into the water. It would draw up enough for Steppin's Pa's fields, encouraging their crops to grow throughout the drought.

I ate my breakfast and drank my milk without once talking to my Ma. It was through fear, not because I was being horrible. Fear of saying something that would give away the secret that I kept locked up in my heart. I could feel my heart as it pumped blood around my now tingling body, so excited was I at seeing Steppin again.

I met him in front of the new fence which his Pa was putting up around their house, once again defining the boundaries of the old Parker place.

He was waiting by their new gate, leaning against it so casually that it could have had been up for longer than just two days. He wore his baseball cap for the first time in ages. His hair shone and his eyes glistened in the morning sun.

I could tell he was happy.

I was too, as I shouted "Hi Steppin" to him and ran across our fields. I held my fishing pole in the air to show that I had brought it as usual. The hook and line waved about until I brought the pole down. I had the bait can in my other hand. I lifted that up too to show him.

He was wearing his oldest pair of jeans. I could see where his mother had smeared suncream over him. It was a ritual he had to put up with every day. I was wearing yesterday's overalls, which were still covered in mud. Steppin's tan was now as deep as mine. He sure was a lot browner than when we first met on the river.

I didn't dare mention yesterday, not right in front of his place.

"Hi, Mickey. How're things?" he asked.

For a second I wondered how I felt.

"All right," I said, beaming a smile at him. "How about you?"

"All right."

"Good," I said, still smiling, remembering yesterday, the best and worst day of my life. The best one ever, because we shared it together. The worst one because of how evil I was. But somehow the evil wasn't very big today, like it was fading away.

"Want to go fishing after we help the Wilkins?" he asked. "Mom's already made lunch and lemonade. She forgot it was your Ma's turn. Your Ma can do it tomorrow if she likes."

"Sh.. sure," I said, answering all of his questions at once. My Ma could do two hundred of her not so nice lunches and I wouldn't mind, provided I could share them all with Steppin.

A beaming smile was fixed on my face like glue. The excitement was clear as crystal in my voice. I definitely wanted to go to the river, our river. It shared our secret.

"Your p.. pole still in your house?" I asked.

"Yep. Want to come in while I get it?"

I wasn't sure. Going inside his house to meet his Ma was not my idea of a good start to the day, after what had happened down by the river yesterday. She was as God-fearing as most of the town. She'd be so mad if she knew what happened, what I'd done to her darling son. It would be worse than anything that had ever happened to me before.

I felt the fingers of my right hand cross my lips. There was no sign to tell her what we had done.

"It's all right," Steppin said. "Mom knows..."

"Kn.. knows... !" I started to say, feeling like I was going to faint. Steppin's Ma knew about yesterday? About what I did!? Oh no! She musn't, she musn't know. If she did then she would... and then they would...

"Knows?" I asked, hearing my voice squeaking like crazy, hoping desperately Steppin hadn't just said what he did.

"Knows how shy you are," he said, opening the gate. "So just say 'hi' and then we'll be off."

"Phew!" I said, sighing, and regaining my balance and mind. Steppin looked at me kind of funny but didn't say anything.

"Okay," I said, so relieved that he hadn't told his mother about what had happened that I wanted to hug him. If he hadn't told her, it meant he wanted it to be a secret too. Our secret.

Still, I thought maybe his Ma could tell what I had done just by looking at me. But if Steppin wanted me to go inside for a minute, then I would, no matter how uneasy I was about it. I followed him across the cracked mud, where his Ma had already started putting out some flowers, to the house, onto the porch and inside.

His Ma was busy washing dishes. She gave us a real friendly smile as we picked up the lunches. I said thank you and hoped she wouldn't notice I was blushing. Then Steppin got out his fishing pole and we set off for the river to hide our gear before going on to help John Wilkins with the rest of the bales left over from the day before.

Down by the river, Steppin took my hand again. He didn't say anything about yesterday and I didn't want to either, in case all the wrong words came out. I thought he couldn't be mad at me, or he wouldn't have given me his hand to hold. It was nice holding hands with him. He was a real friend. I watched his feet as he walked with the usual bouncy step that I liked so much. I tried to copy him, to walk the way he did. He had so much bounce I thought that he must eat springs for breakfast. He laughed at my attempt to walk like he did, which made me laugh too.

Love

After we had hidden our fishing gear, we ran all the way over to Mr Wilkins' farm, to the field we had been working in the day before.

John Wilkins was on his own there. He had already started heaving bales onto the now empty trailer. The bales we had picked up for him the day before were already stacked high in his father's barn.

I don't think he expected us to turn up.

"Hi, there, men. Come back for some more work?" he asked. He looked pleased to see us.

"Yes sir," we both said. He wasn't really old enough for us to call him sir, but it was the least we could do if he called us men.

"Well, we worked so hard yesterday that there's not much more to do. Should finish it this morning."

Why did adults say such stuff? In the mood we were both in we wanted to work all day. I looked at Steppin and then raced him for the nearest bale, trying to pull it to the tractor bed by myself.

He helped me anyway.

I watched as John Wilkins heaved a bale up onto the stack he had already started before we got there.

The remaining bales were odd ones that were out of the regular line the baler had dropped. We had to use more effort pulling them to a point where John drove the tractor up and down the field. He then stopped to help us with the loading.

Getting into the mood of the whole operation, walking or running to a stray straw bale, we soon forgot that John was an adult. He was so good at telling us kids' jokes and funny stories to keep us all going, I thought, as we sweated at a grown man's labour.

The sun and John's stories stretched the morning like elastic, and we constantly ran off ahead of the tractor John was driving as it pulled the trailer with its growing mountain of straw. We would collect together the next four or five bales, and pull them into a group for him to drive up to.

As the bales we ran for were further away, Steppin began to put out his hand for me to hold. I didn't think John would notice in the distance, so I didn't protest. It was a good feeling having Steppin there and having him want me. Otherwise he wouldn't have wanted to hold my hand. Only when John got near with the trailer did I pull it away.

After a couple of hours we heard John calling us to come and get a drink of water. It was hot and we were very sweaty and wanted the rest, so we ran back to him and the water. We drank deep of the large canteen John had brought with him. There wasn't any beer today, but we didn't mind.

After we'd drunk, John pulled a couple of hats from behind his back. "They're for you two men."

They fitted perfectly. They were of equal size and woven with long strands of straw. They weren't stylish, like the sissy ones the girls wore, but perfect for keeping the sun out of our eyes. They would cover our heads from the sun's bright light, so we could work even harder without having to shade our faces, while we dragged the bales to where John was waiting with the tractor. I reckoned John must have taken apart a whole bale of straw to get the long stalks to weave into our hats.

While we rested from the heat, which John insisted we do, Steppin and I sat around the back of the trailer away from the hot sun, leaning together like two bookends. I had my hand in his, not too worried John might see us. He was on the other side tinkering with the tractor engine. We heard him curse softly once or twice.

Our hats were resting on our hunched knees. I found it hard to believe they had been woven with John's large, rough, fingers. His hands looked as if they could never manage to bend the stalks and not break them. They looked more as if they had been made by Steppin's thin, delicate fingers.

Without thinking, I turned my head and kissed Steppin on the right cheek, whispering the same thing I'd told him yesterday.

I loved him.

"I love you too, Mickey," he said, turning to kiss me back.

Just at that moment, John turned the corner of the trailer and saw Steppin kiss me.

Looking up at him as he stood still for a moment, watching us, I became scared. My hand started to sweat in Steppin's, but I didn't take it away as I had done the day before. It was too late for that.

To make it seem equal in John's eyes, I kissed Steppin on his cheek again.

John didn't say anything. I started talking as fast as I could. I told John all about how good Steppin was to me and how he had helped me when I went loony and how he helped me save my fishing pole and how he was the only friend I had because my Pa wouldn't let me have any friends. Steppin was my best friend, my only friend. I loved him. I wouldn't hurt him for the whole world.

All the time I was speaking, John just stood there listening, even when I couldn't get the words out right. He didn't look mad, more kind of curious.

"It's true," Steppin said, when I had finished. "And I love him too." His head nodded, making his long hair swish back and forth. I reached out with my hand and pulled his fringe back off his forehead for him, tucking the loose strands behind his right ear, thinking all the time about how Steppin was so beautiful and I was so ugly.

It was all my fault we had got caught. My fault for letting myself feel that way about him. But I couldn't help it. I just couldn't keep my feelings for Steppin inside any longer. He was my best friend, and I loved him.

I wondered if John had a gun. Then I could kill myself. I knew John would think it had been weird seeing us holding hands while we collected the bales. After what he'd just seen, he'd haul us off to our parents and maybe even the sheriff. If we were lucky, it would just be me, because I was the one who had started it all.

But all he said was, "That's nice."

That was it! Just "That's nice"!

I couldn't believe it.

No horrified looks. No shaking his head in disbelief and wringing his hands, as I had imagined. Nothing about telling our parents or the sheriff or anyone else. I'd told him I loved Steppin and Steppin had told him he loved me and he didn't mind.

I was so happy that I could tell someone else how good I felt whenever I was with Steppin, how my heart sometimes felt like bursting just because I was with him. I had thought I could never tell anyone, because of what they knew about me, all the bad things I had done. Whoever I told was bound to be angry with me, or he'd tell my Pa and my Pa would get real mad. Instead of which, everything was okay.

I leapt up and without thinking hugged John tightly. I was still too short to hug his chest, like I did Steppin's, so I hugged his stomach instead. It wasn't fat, like my Pa's, but thin and hard.

Steppin did the same. Together, we hugged him tight, asking him to swear never to tell anyone because we could get into so much trouble. "Especially Mickey," Steppin said.

John Wilkins was, I decided, my second-best friend.

We had almost finished clearing the field. We set about heaving and pulling more of the straw bales across the fields, albeit more slowly. Neither Steppin or I wanted that morning to end. It made me so glad that John knew our secret and didn't disapprove, or want to stop us loving each other.

Pay

We were both so tired when the field was clear that we said nothing as John drove the tractor back to the farm. We hung our legs over the end of the tailboard of the hay trailer. We kept our hats on. The sun was so strong that they were really needed by the time we finished picking up the bales.

Reaching the Wilkins farmhouse, he told us to wait as we climbed down from the tractor, and he went inside the house.

I thought maybe he was going to give us something for helping him. A cake, or something else nice from the kitchen. Seeing him come back with his father behind him, I almost died. I wanted to run away. He wasn't our friend after all. He had told on us! He had brought us back here so his Pa could deal with us. Mr Wilkins would call the sheriff and have me sent to jail for what we did and what I had told John. I hated John more than anyone in the entire world, even more than my Pa.

Nudging Steppin, I dropped off the trailer and started to walk towards the gate. Steppin stayed where he was. "Come on," I whispered, but he didn't move.

"Where're you going, Mickey?" John called. "Hold on. My Dad wants to thank you."

John's voice sounded friendly enough, but I still didn't trust him. I stopped going anywhere, though.

"Hear you've been right neighborly," Mr Wilkins said. It seemed like he was talking to Steppin and ignoring me like most adults did when they weren't being mad at me. I just stood there, waiting till he had finished, staring at the ground. I was holding my boots firmly in my hands, afraid Mr Wilkins might take one and whack me with it. They had been too sweaty to work in, so I had put them on the hay trailer until we'd finished. Steppin's feet weren't as rough as mine, so he wore his boots while we worked. His feet would really smell, I thought.

I kept my head bowed waiting for Mr Wilkins to finish and let us go. I knew he didn't like having me around. I was a bad boy who wasn't allowed on his land. I wanted to run from his yard, across the field we'd just worked in, run back to the river, to hide from him and everyone else. I was happy there; it was the only place I was happy except the field we'd just come from.

"Thanks, boys," Mr Wilkins said. Boys, he'd said. He meant me too. Maybe he wasn't mad at me after all.

I saw Mr Wilkins' boots approach my bare feet and kind of half looked up. "You're not such a bad lad, are you, Mickey?" I heard Mr Wilkins say to the top of my head, and felt his hand ruffling my black curly hair.

It was a long time since any adult had done that to me. I thought maybe he was playing with me, trying to make me mad, or maybe he really was mad at me. But it didn't feel like it. "N.. no, sir," I mumbled, shaking my head slowly.

"Here, this is for your help, but don't expect it every time."

He took my hand and placed something in it, closing my hand in his huge fist.

"Thank you, sir," I said, just clear enough for him to hear.

He did the same to Steppin. "Good to have you as a neighbor, son" he said, ruffling his golden head of hair like he had ruffled mine. The sun had worked hard on bleaching all of the brown out of it over the weeks we'd fished, swam, or just played together. I didn't like Mr Wilkins doing that, but said nothing.

We looked into our hands. A whole dollar each! We were rich!

I couldn't believe it. He knew what I'd done to his nephew. He knew nobody trusted me, nobody wanted me around. Yet he still gave me a dollar. And John hadn't told him about me and Steppin. I was all confused. Leaving the Wilkins place, I started running as fast as I could over the field toward the river. I kept thinking about the dollar and what I'd done. How could Mr Wilkins hand out a dollar to the boy who'd stabbed his nephew with a knife? I didn't understand it. I could have killed him.

"Hey, slow down, Mickey," Steppin called. "I'm getting a stitch." I kept on running, but he called again, so I stopped and waited for him to catch up with me. Then we started walking instead of running.

"What's the matter, Mickey?" Steppin asked, seeing that I looked like I might start crying again. I couldn't tell him not yet. I hadn't figured it out myself.

"N.. nothin'," I said.

"A dollar!" Steppin said. "If we work every day, we'll be rich!"

I didn't say anything. I was still thinking about Jamie, Mr Wilkins' nephew. He was one of the victims of my real crime, except I didn't always see it that way. I couldn't figure it out. Why had Mr Wilkins been so kind to me, of all kids?

Sometimes I felt rotten for what I had done to Jamie. Except it wasn't my fault. Jamie had been the one to try and grab the knife off me, after I'd slashed the gas-station kid on the face. He was just going to be the first, I'd shouted.

I reckon it was brave of Jamie, trying to get it off me.

I wished I was that brave. I'd been a coward with Sally Ives and with a knife in my hand I was still a coward. I was afraid to put it down, afraid they'd all come after me. I had it in my bag to go fishing that day. Then they started calling me names and I lost my head. I got the knife out and started waving it about, cornering a dozen kids in the classroom. I was going to do them all in, I screamed, for what they said about me. And I meant it. I really meant it.

The gas-station kid tried to jump me from the side, but I was real strong, spun him off my back and cut him. It wasn't bad. I got him in the face, right across his cheek. When that happened, none of the other kids did anything. The girls started bawling. Some of the boys were whimpering and they all looked real scared.

All except for Jamie. He said if I didn't put the knife down, he'd get the Principal. That made me even madder. I told him I'd do the Principal in too, if he came in.

Then he started calling out "Help!" and calling the Principal's name. I told him to shut up or I'd hurt him. I really did want to hurt him, all of them, and at the same time I didn't. So I just stood there, holding my knife and shaking it at them.

But Jamie hollered louder and louder. I heard the door open behind me. At the same time Jamie rushed at me and tried to get the knife. I just raised my hand and brought it right down. It went right through his hand and out the other side. I was looking at it and thinking I was sorry I'd done it and at the same time I was glad. Then the Principal grabbed my arm and I dropped the knife. It was a good thing too, I reckoned afterwards, or else I'd have stabbed him as well.

There was blood all over the place, but Jamie wasn't hurt that bad. They took him to the doctor and he had to wear a bandage for a month. All the kids at school said he was a hero, or so I heard. That was the last time I saw him. The last time I went to that place.

"Hey, Mickey, come on! Everything's okay," Steppin said as we walked towards the river. He put his arm across my shoulder and pulled me towards him. It felt so good having him so close. I slipped my arm up around his shoulder and we walked to the river like that.

8

Sleepover

Mom says you can sleep over at our house tonight if you want to," Steppin announced just after we had started to fish.

"Wh.. what?" I asked, not sure I'd heard what he just said.

"Mom says," he repeated slowly, turning to face me, "that you can sleep over at our place tonight. That is if your Ma don't mind, she said. I told her about you never going to sleep over with anyone, so she said..."

"You .t.. told her about me...? About us?" I couldn't believe what I was hearing. It was a secret, our secret.

"No, not that, Mickey. Just that you never had a sleep-over invitation. That's all."

Steppin had worried me a bit then. What if he had told her about us! John Wilkins was the only adult who knew. I wished we hadn't told him now. He might tell his father, who would tell my Pa and the sheriff and then everyone would know.

Then I thought about sleeping over in Steppin's house. Steppin and me sharing the same room? Maybe even the same bed. I got that funny feeling again, about sleeping next to Steppin all night long. Snuggling up next to him all warm and tight. Maybe we wouldn't wear any clothes or anything.

I wondered why Steppin's parents would invite me into their home, place their trust in me, knowing everything about me like they did.

Then I thought it was a trick, it had to be. A trick to get me to confess everything, especially what I'd done to their son. I just knew it was. Steppin was in on it because he really was horrified about what I done!

"We could sleep in the barn, like you said you do a lot," Steppin said when I didn't say anything.

I thought about it. It wouldn't be the same. One barn was pretty much like another. Half the fun of sleeping over was discovering what toys kids had and how their houses looked. Or so I thought, anyway.

Or what pet names parents had for their kids.

But the barn sounded safer, away from his Ma and Pa. "Okay," I said, "the b.. barn."

"Your parents won't mind?" Steppin asked.

I thought about it. I just knew my Pa would say no. Ma wouldn't mind. Maybe if I just asked her, it would be all right.

"It'll b.. be okay."

"Great," he said. "Now let's fish."

*   *   *

"What're you doing?" I whispered to Steppin, who was lying next to me under his blanket.

We had made two cosy beds of straw from a loose bale and put our blankets on top. Two mats of straw put under our bottom blankets formed our pillows, so their stalks wouldn't get up our noses or into our ears as we slept. I'd tried to get to sleep, but was too excited to keep my eyes closed.

We had got permission from Steppin's Ma to have our sleepover in the barn, on account of my 'shyness'. Steppin explained it to his Ma without making me blush. That was nice and kind, I thought. She had said okay, after he said I'd told my Ma. Ma hadn't been too happy about it, but I begged and told her how good I'd been in the last few weeks. It was true, so she let me go.

We'd talked for hours about all sorts of things after we'd made our beds, but we hadn't talked about kissing or how much we loved each other. I didn't want to because I was beginning to think again that sort of feeling was all wrong. And I was sure Steppin had changed his mind. He hadn't held my hand all evening. I wanted to hold his, but I was afraid to do so.

"What?" Steppin said in a sort of hoarse voice.

For some reason he hadn't heard what I had whispered to him, even though he was right next to me. I don't think he was listening.

"What're you doing?" I said a little louder.

"Nothing. Just... practising."

"P.. practisin'?" I asked.

"Yeah."

"Practisin' what?" I asked, sitting up. The moonlight was strong and I could see Steppin clearly, lying there with his blanket drawn up to his chin

"Practising. Like this." He threw back his blanket. He'd pushed down his pajamas and had the thin delicate fingers of his right hand on his peter. It was much bigger now, long and hard. As I watched, he rubbed it up and down, like he was trying to pull it off or stretch it to make it bigger.

My peter got hard too, sometimes, but I'd never rubbed it the way Steppin was rubbing his. It looked painful, seeing the way he pulled on it like that and the way he frowned. It was at least twice as big as it had been before. Even when mine was really hard, I didn't think it was that big. It wasn't fair, but I tried not to feel jea

"Can I?" I said.

"Sure."

I reached over and gently touched his peter. Steppin was right; it felt really good.

"Mickey," Steppin said.

"Yeah?"

"I meant have a go with your own."

"Oh," I said. "S.. sorry." I was disappointed. I liked holding Steppin's. Now he was mad at me.

But he wasn't. He saw how I felt.

"I'm sorry, Mickey," he said. "You can do it next time. Show me yours."

I was a bit ashamed to, because mine was so small. But I couldn't say no to Steppin. I pushed my blanket down and opened my pajama pants. My peter was already almost hard. I put my fingers round it and started rubbing the way I had seen Steppin doing. He was right. It felt real good. I got this funny trembling feeling all the way through my body.

I stopped and looked at Steppin. "Wow!" I said.

"Yeah," he smiled. "Wow, all right." He was leaning over and looking at mine. "Yours is thicker," he said.

It was, but his was longer.

He put his hand on my peter. It felt good too, but kind of different from when I did it. Then I put my hand on his and rubbed a little. I liked the feeling of his warm peter, like it was both hard and soft at the same time.

Then we both rubbed our own.

"See who finishes first," Steppin said.

I didn't know what he meant, so I just kept rubbing as long as he did. We both got faster and faster and the funny feeling inside grew and grew until my whole body was tingling and I kind of exploded, like the times I lost my head, except this time it was the most wonderful feeling I'd ever had.

The feeling was just going away when I heard Steppin beside me making groaning noises, like he was in pain. His whole body jerked a bit and some sticky stuff came out of his peter. That made look down at mine. It was a bit damp too. I thought it must be piss.

"You win," said Steppin.

"I do?"

"Yeah, you finished first."

"S.. Steppin," I said. "That was amazin'."

"You never done it before?" Steppin asked.

I shook my head. I still felt kind of strange. Like I felt after I'd kissed Steppin, but even more so.

"I done it a few times," Steppin said, "but always on my own. I like it better with you."

He stood up and walked over to the door, the one which opened onto the yard below. "Got to piss," he said.

"S.. so do I."

It was naughty to piss into his Pa's yard, but Steppin was the one who had suggested it. I couldn't really think of Steppin as being naughty. But he was the one who stole the candy from Mr Johnson's store. So he must be naughty sometimes.

As we pissed out into the yard, I asked Steppin how he knew about practising. He told me other boys had told him about it in the place where he last lived. Then his Ma had caught him in the bathroom practising one day. She'd told his Pa and his Pa had explained about babies and where they came from. "It's just like a bull covering a cow," he said. I kind of knew that anyway. I just hadn't thought about it much. And I'd never seen a bull practising before.

I thought maybe it was wrong to practise and Steppin said his parents didn't seem to mind. He wasn't sure about doing it with other boys, though.

"Wh.. what about girls?" I asked.

He shook his head. Not until he got married, he said.

I hoped he wouldn't get married for a long, long time.

It was cold and soon as we'd finished peeing and shaking ourselves dry, we'd rushed back to the blankets. I snuggled down right into mine, trying to get warm and trying to get some of the good feeling of practising back.

It had sure made me hot and sweaty, I thought, as I got warm again. I wondered if it would always be like that, or was it just because I was learning how to do it. I'd do it again one day, hopefully with Steppin. Maybe he want to do it to me. I wondered if that would make it feel different.

I was still trying to get comfortable when I heard Steppin call my name.

"Yeah, Steppin," I whispered back.

"You can snuggle up to me if you want to," he said. "It'll be warmer."

"You don't m.. mind?" I asked.

"Course not," he said.

"Okay," I said, as I pulled his blanket over me. I was lying right next him, with my head using his shoulder and part of his chest as a pillow. He had his left arm around my shoulder, resting his thin fingers on my upper arm.

I had my left arm and hand across his stomach. Steppin had said it was alright to put it there. I really liked lying close to him like that. He was warm and I could feel his heartbeat.

With just my chin poking out over the blanket, which itched, we settled down to try to sleep. My only remaining concern was that my long, ugly curls were next to his beautiful skin. I didn't want my ugliness to affect him.

"All right, Mickey?" he asked, gently nuzzling my head with his chin, just in case I had fallen asleep already.

"All right, Steppin," I replied, nodding in the darkness.

"Good," he said. He lifted his head off the straw pillow for a second, moved it a bit and then laid it back down as he settled. We could have both shared the straw pillow, but I preferred to have my head against his shoulder as I looked over the blanket covering his chest.

Then he lifted his head off the pillow, leant forward and kissed the side of my head, with its long black curls, just like my Ma used to do every night. But she hadn't done for years.

"Good night, Mickey," he said.

I don't know why it made me want to cry, but I bit my lip and stopped myself before I could cry a single tear.

"Good night Steppin," I whispered, carefully breathing out the words so he wouldn't know I was upset. Then, closing my eyes, I said the same three words as before.

I was falling asleep by then, but I swear I heard him repeat them back to me.

Breakfast

I woke to see the dawn sun filtering into the hayloft, spreading dusty beams of light through the gaps in the rough, slatted door that sealed out the cold night.

Lying in the blankets next to Steppin, I felt warm and cosy. It felt like all the perfect mornings I had ever imagined, all rolled into one.

My head was still on Steppin's chest, and my chin was just above the top blanket, which had done its best to keep us both warm throughout the night.

But I reckoned it was the combined warmth of our bodies that kept the chill off.

I breathed out an expanding cloud of frosty mist over and across the top of the blanket and toward the barn wall.

I still had my arm across Steppin's stomach, which was warm beneath my fingers. He had a nice, slim belly. He wasn't fat, not like some of the boys I knew.

The dawn's fresh atmosphere surrounded me and Steppin as we lay there in the loft. My second cloudy breath settled on the top of the straw bales that were around us like the walls of a fort.

It was magical, just like a fairy tale when the prince woke up from his hundred-year sleep. Or was it a princess? I didn't care, but just continued to enjoy the feeling.

With Steppin beside me, and knowing that he felt as I did, I was happy just to let the magic continue to weave itself over us.

"Morning Mickey," I heard him say in a quiet voice.

I hoped I hadn't disturbed him by twisting my head about to look around the hayloft, which I still thought of as a place of security and protection.

I also hoped he hadn't woken up before he was ready to wake naturally, just like I used to when I slept in the barn. I craned my head to look round at him.

"Morning, Steppin," I said. "Sleep well?"

"Uh-huh," he said, taking his arm from around my shoulder and, with the other, lifting it right above his head. With a really long yawn, he pushed his legs straight out, like a cat did when it stretched its entire body, before collapsing in the blankets again.

"Better?" I asked, as he put his arm around me again.

"Yep! Sure is," he said.

"Good. I.. I love you, S.. Steppin," I said quickly while the thought was still there. Each time I said it, it was easier. "I love you too, Mickey," he said, squeezing my shoulder toward him a bit and lifting himself up to kiss the side of my forehead.

Nothing could be better than this. If I had died right there and then, next to him, in the hayloft, it would have been all right.

It was the perfect start to a perfect morning.

"Pa said he would bring some breakfast out to us," Steppin said, as we lay in the warm blankets talking. The small door to the hayloft was now open, letting in the sun. It was at an angle, so it didn't shine directly in our eyes.

I had rushed over to open it, and then rushed to get back under the blankets as it was cold outside.

As I snuggled down with my head on his chest again, Steppin said I was cold. I didn't see how I could be. He felt warm enough.

As we waited for the sun's rays to warm up the hayloft, and for his Pa to bring breakfast, Steppin asked what I wanted to do that day.

Seeing as how I was sleeping over, I got first choice of the day's activities. I was his guest, but I said he could choose. He said no, it was up to me.

"Honeycombs," I said.

"Honeycombs?"

"I know where we can get some." I didn't want to tell him where. He'd find out anyway.

"Okay," he said. "We'll pick honeycombs."

"Boys!" we suddenly heard from below. "I've got your breakfast."

We jumped up and rushed down the ladder to where Steppin's Pa held two steaming breakfast bowls he had carefully carried out to us, making sure he didn't spill a drop. I liked to think this was so we'd get to have a full bowl each.

Steppin's Pa was as bright and cheerful as Steppin was. That was logical, I thought, because Steppin was his son.

"Morning, Pop. Thanks," Steppin said as he took his bowl from his Pa and a spoon from his Pa's trouser pocket. His Pa didn't seem to mind Steppin taking the spoon without asking.

"Morning, Golden Boy," Steppin's Pa said as he watched his son take the bowl of breakfast. He tussled Steppin's hair some, then smoothed it out from the tangle it was in from sleeping in the straw with me.

Golden Boy!

That was a nice name for Steppin's Pa to call him. It made my heart go thump to hear him called that.

"Good morning, s.. sir," I said shyly, as I took the bowl he offered me. I waited as he brought the spoon out of his pocket and gave me that too.

"Morning, Mickey. Did you sleep well?"

"Oh yes, s.. sir, I did, v.. very well," I said, nodding my head and speaking in my polite voice. He didn't reach forward and tussle my hair or smooth it down. I didn't blame him. I wouldn't have if I were him.

Steppin's Pa had called him Golden Boy! Wow! That was real nice.

"Well, come on boys, hurry up and eat your breakfast. And get some clothes on or you'll catch your deaths."

"Yes, sir," we both said as he left the barn so we could eat our breakfast.

"Oh, Steppin," his Pa said, turning back for a second. "Your ma wants some eggs, fetch them in will you, please?"

"Yes, sir," Steppin said.

We knew better than to believe we'd catch cold from spending five minutes in the damp air of the open barn, so we took our time to eat our breakfast. Besides, the doors were open, letting in the sunshine. We were sitting on a straw bale which would soon be breakfast for the cows, trying to outdo each other with the most disgusting slurping sounds we could make while wolfing down the contents of the bowl.

We were soon warm enough and our bellies full. I didn't think we'd catch anything, not even a cold. We might catch a fever from the piping hot food slopping about inside us, but from the cold morning? Never.

"Want some milk?" Steppin asked when I had finished. As soon as I had, I put the bowl besides me on the bale and belched and farted loudly. It was my regular morning habit when my Ma and Pa weren't around.

"Sure," I said, opening my mouth and letting out the air inside my stomach at the same time. It made my voice go all sort of deep for a moment.

"Phew!!" Steppin said, waving the smell of my fart away. "You stink!"

I could tell he was being funny about it.

"Thanks. It was a good one, wasn't it?"

"It sure was. Bet you can't do another like that one again!"

I won the bet.

* * *

"Hey? Stop that! I want to get some too!" I yelled as Steppin squirted me with a stream of milk for the third time. He was squeezing the cow's tit at me, just about making me spill the bowl of milk that I was trying to fill to the brim.

We had decided that fresh was best, so had sneaked up to the nearest unsuspecting cow and started to milk her. That was until Steppin started to fool around.

I sprayed him right back, right under the cow that was standing there ignoring the fight over her milk. Soon we were covered in milk dribbles and called a truce. The cow didn't seem to mind who milked her, or where it went when it left her udder, over us or in our bowls. She probably thought it was just an early milking and was glad to relieve the pressure.

Taking our bowls back up the loft was difficult. Steppin spilled a little of his. So I did too, to even them both up.

We supped the warm milk as we talked and dressed.

As I pulled my boots on, I set to thinking that it was weird that there was all that blood pumping inside me, so full of evil, yet when I was practising, I had felt so good.

Steppin said it was my blood that made my peter stand up. So maybe there wasn't so much evil in me after all. Maybe there was just a little good left in me to let me practise, I thought, as we climbed down the ladder.

"Hang on a minute while I get the egg basket," Steppin said as he came down the ladder. But instead of going into the house for it, he picked it up from the barn door. His Pa had left there for him. His Pa had been real polite too, in asking him to get the eggs. Not like my Pa.

"Here, you hold this while I put them in," Steppin said as he handed me the basket.

"I'd better not, Steppin," I said, shaking my head. "I'll just drop them all over the place. I always do."

"No you won't, Mickey. Just hold the basket real tight."

He put his hands underneath some chickens who were too lazy to be scratching in the coop that early in the morning and brought out the precious eggs. I was real nervous as he started putting them into the basket I was holding. I gripped the handle real hard, not wanting to drop it and spill the eggs.

When he plain insisted I have a go at getting an egg myself, I was real nervous, sure I'd drop it before it got to the basket.

"Oh Steppin, I'm going to drop it, I'm sure I am!" I said, thinking of all the other times I was told to get the eggs from our chickens, but ended up with nothing. They kept pecking me and I dropped more eggs than I ever put into the basket. Pa used to get real mad at me, he said I was the only boy in the world who couldn't pick up an egg a hen had just laid.

"No, you won't, not if you move real slow," he said, watching me closely with the egg in my hand, while putting another two eggs he got into the basket.

"I'm going to drop it, Steppin."

"No, you're not."

I clenched my fist so tight I squashed it instead.

"S.. see!" I said, throwing the mashed remains to the floor in a temper. "I'm no good at anything! My P.. Pa's right. I'm plain d.. dumb and stupid."

"No, you're not," Steppin said. He picked up the egg-shell, looked at it and said, "It wasn't your fault, Mickey. It was the shell. It was too thin." He showed me it. "It was the chicken's fault. Come on, I've got all the rest."

"S.. stupid chicken," I said to the bird where I'd got the egg from. She just clucked to herself. "It wasn't my fault! You're d.. dumber than I am, chicken!," I shouted, and followed Steppin out of the coop.

Suncream

Despite me saying to Steppin's Ma that I didn't need it, she insisted on covering me in suncream.

I was standing, as Steppin was, in their kitchen with my overalls down around my ankles while she smeared my chest. Steppin had put a fresh pair of jeans on. My overalls hadn't been washed in days.

Steppin's Ma was ever so gentle rubbing the suncream on. She made sure my arms were covered and even put some under my armpits. I think she did that because Steppin told her that we used to lie back on the riverbank and use our hands like pillows while basking. It tickled as she worked it in. I couldn't help but smile at her. It was nice, as she was.

She smiled back at me.

"Mickey...?" Steppin's Ma asked quietly as she started on the top of my shoulders.

"Yes ma'am?" I said.

"Steppin said you were bullied at...," she hesitated.

"Ma!" Steppin hissed, as he realized she was going to say the one word that was guaranteed to send me loony.

She looked at Steppin in a sort of disapproving way. "He said you were called names because you had a bit of trouble with your numbers and reading books."

"They called me D.. Dumbo!" I said. It made me think of the elephant in the cartoon, the one with the big ears. I had big ears and I was dumb too. "They m.. made fun of the way I t.. talk too," I said. "I hate them."

I saw Steppin breathe a sigh of relief. She hadn't said that word after all. I felt relieved too. But a bit mad at Steppin for telling his Ma what I'd told him. I looked at him real mean for a second.

"You're not dumb, Mickey," his Ma said. "It just takes you a little more time than the other kids. You'll learn to count really well and read just as well as the other children."

"That's n.. not what the t.. teacher says," I said. Part of me didn't like Steppin's Ma going on at me about that place, but part of me didn't mind it. It wasn't the way my Ma and Pa talked to me about it.

"Maybe things'll be easier when you go back with Steppin," she said.

Even the thought of going back there made me a bit mad. "I ain't never goin' back," I said, shaking my head fiercely. "N.. never!"

I didn't think Steppin's Ma'd give up talking about that place just like that. I just wanted to get out of there and started walking to the door. But I forgot my overalls were half off and I tripped up and would have fallen if Steppin's Ma hadn't caught me and pulled me upright again.

"Steady, Mickey. I haven't finished with the suncream yet," she said, turning me round so we were face to face.

"Mickey," she started to say, as she looked at Steppin, stopped and then started again. "I had a bit of trouble with my numbers and reading when I was your age. But, do you know what my mother did when she realized?"

I shook my head. I didn't want to hear what she had to say, but I couldn't be rude, not to Steppin's Ma.

"My mother got me some books and taught me herself all that I'd missed out. She got me counting real good and reading stories too."

"I like the one about the d.. dragon and the prince," I said without thinking.

"You mean the princess, Mickey? But never mind. If you like, you can look at Steppin's books and I'll help you with your numbers. And Steppin will help, won't you?" she said, turning to him.

"Sure thing, Mickey!" Steppin said with a real nice smile on his face, like it was a nice surprise. He probably never even thought of what his Ma had said. I could see all his teeth right to the back. "Yeah, you and I can learn together!"

"I ain't never going back there!" I said, but I wasn't as mad as I was before. I just said it like my mind was made up and nobody, not even Steppin, could change it.

Steppin's Ma didn't say anything to that. She probably thought I'd want some more time to think about it. Instead she just got on with covering me with cream until I started going all red and she looked down and saw what has happening to my peter. It must be her, I thought. It wasn't me.

"Maybe you'd better help Mickey finish off, Steppin," she said, standing up. "I've got work to do. Go out onto the porch, and remember to put the top back on."

"Yes Mom," Steppin said.

I shuffled out onto the porch, with Steppin following me with the cream. But when Steppin rubbed my chest with cream, it was worse. My peter was standing straight out, nearly poking through my underpants. It was as hard as when we were in the barn. I wanted to rub it again, but couldn't, because his Ma would surely see.

Steppin noticed and smiled. I couldn't help but smile back. I sort of forgave him for telling on me. But I wasn't going back to that place, though I liked the idea of being as brainy as all the other kids. Then I could show Sally Ives for the stupid girl she really was.

"Here, do my back will you, Mickey?"

"Sh.. sure, Steppin," I said taking the suncream as he turned round. I squeezed a long trail out over his shoulders.

"Hey, that's cold!"

"S.. Sorry," I said. "I'll rub it in quick, then you'll warm up." I started rubbing the cream in circles across his shoulders and down over his arms.

I liked being able to touch him like this. I forgave him completely for telling his Ma about me and that place as I rubbed. I squeezed some on my hands and started rubbing it on his back, and then on his ribs, doing them really slow, rubbing him like his Ma rubbed me.

I started to feel all hot even though we weren't in the sun yet, but still on the porch. It was rubbing Steppin that made me hot.

I whispered to him really quiet in his ear, "I love you, Steppin. I'm not mad at you any more for telling your Ma."

He turned round and shook his hair back over his ear, a smile on his face that made me even hotter inside. I couldn't help but give him as big a smile as he was giving me.

"I love you too," he said, leaning forward to kiss me on the lips, real gentle like. I stared at his open eyes when he did it. I was still hot. My peter was so hard it hurt.

Steppin insisted on holding my hand as we walked off down the dirt road. I didn't look back to see if his Ma was looking.

I didn't know if what she'd said about being slow with numbers and reading and having trouble like I did was all made up, to make me feel better. Maybe it was true. It didn't matter. I wasn't ever going back to that place. Never again.

9

Honey

I had told Steppin that the honeycombs came from nature. It was true. But I didn't tell him till we got there that nature had put the honeycombs inside the beehives in the Widow Vanden's garden. Then he wasn't sure about sneaking in. "Aren't you afraid of her witching powers?" he asked.

The truth was, I was afraid. I'd been more and more afraid the closer we got to town. But I couldn't tell Steppin that. I'd wanted to show him something special and this was it.

"Her p.. powers?" I said, thinking real quick. "She can't get anyone..." I had to think real hard about what to say next, "who's in love, cause love conquers all b.. bad things, even witches!"

Steppin looked like he didn't believe me, but he said, "Okay, if you're sure."

"Sh.. sure I'm sure," I said. "But you'd b.. better hold my hand, so as we're protected."

Before we sneaked through a hole in the fence I looked up at the house, but I didn't see anything. I knew the Widow always spent the morning shopping and watching out for boys on the streets who she wanted to torture.

Anyhow, I knew Steppin wasn't afraid. He'd been the one who'd squashed the toad with the rock on our way into town. And he showed me how to squash beetles between your fingers. He wanted to show me that he could be bad too.

The beetles exploded and sprayed themselves all over my hands. They smelt terrible.

"Yuck," I said to Steppin. "That stinks."

"Sure does, Mickey. Remind you of anything?" he asked, turning sniffing the air around me.

I laughed and pushed him over on the grass. He struggled to get up without making any noise, as I kept pushing on him again and again. Eventually we kept going on our way to the Widow's as I wiped off the gunk from the beetles on my overalls.

We ran across the grass right up to the hives. The Widow's garden was a mess. It used to be all overgrown flowers and grass, but they had all died in the drought. I held Steppin's hand to ward off her witching. I'd once hear Pa say she couldn't cast any spells, but I didn't believe him. Everyone knew she was a witch.

When we opened a hive, the bees began buzzing around us in protest, intent on defending their prize. I ignored them. I had been stung before, and knew it wasn't too painful. Certainly not as painful as my Black Emptiness.

Steppin was clearly nervous with the bees flying about him, even though he had said he was used to stings too. I didn't believe him, but didn't call him a liar.

"Come on," I whispered as we crept toward the fence on our way out of the garden, each of us holding a honeycomb. We weren't holding hands any more, cause we were too scared we might drop the honeycombs.

"You, boys! What're you doing in my garden?"

It was the Widow, coming in the front gate. She looked tall and evil and was dressed all in black. It was her witching dress.

"Run!" I shouted at Steppin as she started walking toward us. I ran as fast as I could for the hole in the fence, holding the comb tight against the front of my overalls. I wasn't going to panic and drop it. Steppin was right behind me, running just as fast.

As I pushed through the fence I looked back and saw that the Widow had stopped chasing us. She was staring at the beehive, the one we'd taken the honeycombs from. I hadn't put the roof back on properly.

"You thieves!" she screamed at us. "You thieves!" Steppin came out on the road and we started running as fast as could back home.

"Look what you've done to my hive! I'll get you for this!" I could hear the Widow shouting. She had a mighty big voice. "I'll make you pay. I knows who you are! Hear me? I knows who you are!" she screamed at our backs.

Steppin sure could run, I thought, as I followed him down the dusty road. He might look skinny and weak but he could run faster than I could. Even while we were running, I really liked watching him and thinking he was my friend and we loved each other. That made stealing the honeycombs not so bad.

Then I thought about all the bad things the Widow could do to us if she was really mean. She could cast a sleeping spell on Steppin, like the witch did on Snow White or who-ever it was.

Mind you, I thought, if she did, I could ride up on a white charger into Steppin's overgrown farmyard, after hacking my way through the forest that had kept him and his beauty from the world for so long.

I would climb up into the hayloft and find him asleep, bewitched on a bed covered by his long golden hair, which had kept him warm in his hundred-year sleep.

With a kiss on his delicate thin red lips, I would then waken the prince.

And we'd be happy ever after again.

When we were out of breath, we stopped and looked back. The widow wasn't following us.

"D.. don't worry about her," I told Steppin. "She's b.. blind as a bat. My Pa says it's a w.. wonder she can drive her t.. truck the way she is."

"Are you sure?" he asked. He looked kind of scared. Maybe he was just breathless, but it made me feel good to think of him being scared, so as he would need me to protect him.

"Sure," I said.

"Good."

"Anyhow, we did n.. nothin' wrong in taking her combs," I said. "She's always chasing boys and t.. telling on them. Then she expects all the boys to l.. load things off and on her truck and she n.. never gives them a tip, not even a th.. thank you. She's mean and she's horrible and I hate her."

"Me too," said Steppin, though I think it was just to make me feel good. I did feel good, seeing as how I was with him and the honey. All we had to do now was eat it and spend the rest of the day alone together.

I loved Steppin. I really did.

Prince

Sitting on the riverbank, eating honey. It's good. I like looking at Steppin. I don't care if he sees. He's like a Prince in a picture book, handsome and fair hair and all. I bet girls love him.

But I'm a boy. That's what makes it bad. I love him and he loves me. That's wrong. I know, but I can't do nothin' about it.

He's so kind and beautiful. I want to reach out and stroke his hair. But he don't like it. Maybe I can get to do it another time.

I'm ugly. Steppin says I don't look bad at all, but he just says that to make me feel good. I hate the way I look. My ears stick out and my hair is all over the place. I got a pigeon chest. My legs and arms are too long. I look like some kind of big insect.

People laugh at me, even when they think they're being kind. They're not. They just make it worse. Even Ma and Pa think I look bad. I bet when I was born they wanted to send me away, to an orphanage just for ugly kids. Ever since I got into trouble they knew they were right. But it was too late, they couldn't get rid of me.

All the kids feel the same. Except Steppin. And that's only cause he don't know everythin'. He don't know what I did with the knife. If he did, he wouldn't stick around. He wouldn't love me. He'd hate me too.

I don't know what's going to happen to him in that place. He looks awful delicate, like a girl. All the bullies are much stronger than him. Except he's clever. He knows what he's doing. He's not dumb and he's not a coward like me. Maybe he'll find a way not to be bullied. Just as long as he don't let them find out he's my friend.

Leastways Sally Ives won't bully him. He wouldn't let her.

I won't have anyone to play with when he goes to that place. He won't want to know me when he gets to know the other kids. I wish I had someone else, like a brother. But Ma got real mad at me when I asked her for one. Even a sister. That was years ago. Even if Ma and Pa had another kid now, it would be too late. He'd only be a baby and I couldn't wait for him to get to my age.

I remember I once told her and Pa I'd look after the kid. I'd make sure he never messed the house up. I'd feed him and change his diapers. I'd do everything. But Pa didn't like the idea. He looked at me real hard and then at Ma and said "I ain't having another like him around my house."

I hated Pa for saying that. I've always hated him. Ma too. Sometimes she's good to me, but most of the time she never wants me around. Except to clean my room or wash my face or things like that. Like Pa, who don't want me to help him. They both wish I'd never been born. I hate them. I hate them.

Comb finished. It was good. Belch.

"I'm goin' to s.. stretch out, Steppin." He's still eating his.

Lying on the grass, sun on my back, butt stickin' in the air. I like my butt. I see it in the bedroom mirror, curving round, sloping down to the rear of my knees. Round and firm. When I clench it, it makes me walk like a penguin.

Maybe my Ma wanted a girl instead of me. A girl wouldn't be so dumb. A girl would look good. She'd like a girl. Pa wouldn't mind a girl so much. He wouldn't get so mad at a girl. Maybe I was meant to be a girl and something went wrong. That's how come I love Steppin and he loves me. Girls like boys, especially if they look like Steppin.

Maybe I'll still be a girl. Maybe I'll grow tits and my peter'll disappear. I'll get a girl's thing instead. Then the boys'll make even more fun of me.

I don't want to be a girl. I'd rather be dead.

"It's not fair!"

"What's wrong, Mickey?"

He looks at me. He looks so good. I can't tell him. I can't tell him I'm afraid I'm a girl. I'm not really, but... But I couldn't explain it right and he wouldn't understand.

"N.. nothing. S.. sorry, Steppin."

He finishes off his comb, wipes his mouth. I sit up and wipe it for him. He smiles. It looks really good, his smile. I can't stop myself kissing him, my honey lips on his. I kind of want to do more, but don't know what.

"Steppin?"

"Yeah?"

"You w.. won't ever go away, will you?"

I want him to say never. Never, Mickey. I'll never leave you!

"From here? Don't know. Depends if Pop can make a go of it."

"And if he d.. don't?"

"I don't know, Mickey. We might have to sell up and go somewhere else."

"But my P.. Pa is doing okay."

"He doesn't have all the debts my father has. He borrowed money from the bank for the tractor and the land and everything."

I think of Steppin leaving. It really makes me sad.

"Don't worry, Mickey. I won't leave, not if I can help it."

"You could s.. sleep in our barn. If your Pa has to leave the f.. farm, you can stay in our barn. I'll give you my big b.. blanket and my pillow. Pa won't let you into the house, but I'll b.. bring you breakfast every day, forever. Just like your Pa did for us."

If he slept in our barn every night, I could take him his breakfast, waking him up ever so gently. When he opened his eyes, I could call him Golden Boy and ruffle his hair for him, like his Pa.

"Thanks, Mickey." He takes my hand and squeezes it. I hope he never lets it go. I think I can see a tear in his eye.

"That's okay, S., Steppin. Any time." I want to say Golden Boy but he might not like it.

"Mickey." He don't say nothin' more. He leans over and kisses me again. He's still holding my hand and squeezing it tight. Our lips almost stick together.

We got to stop sometime. I stand up and say "Wh.. what about a swim?" Partly because I want to cool off and partly because I've got that funny feeling again. I want to see him with no clothes on. I want to see his peter again.

"There you are! I told you I'd find you. I'm going to make you pay."

The Widow. Running over the fields. Screamin' and shoutin'. She wants Steppin and me. We stole her honey. She's goin' to come and catch us. I don't think she's goin' to make a spell. She just wants to beat us. Or she's goin' to take us to the sheriff. Or to my Pa.

Running as fast as I can. Running away from the river. Running away from the Widow. Running away from my Pa. Running away from a beating. Running away from that place. Running away from the kids. Running away from Sally Ives.

Running, running, running, running.

It's all over. She must have seen me and Steppin. Kissing like that. She's going to tell on us. Pa's goin' to beat me. He's goin' to lock me up, send me away. I'll never see Steppin again. Never, never, never.

They'll punish Steppin too. It's all my fault. I took him to the Widow's. I made him steal. I kissed him. I told him I loved him. I made him do all these things. His Ma and Pa'll hate me. They won't let me see Steppin again. My Ma and Pa won't let me see anyone again. I'll spend the rest of my life here, alone on this river. I'll never be happy again.

I'm bad. I'm bad. I'm bad. I can't speak right, I can't think right. I can't do nothin' right. Nobody likes me. Nobody wants me. Not even Steppin. Not when the Widow catches up with him and his Ma and Pa learn what I made him do. He'll hate me too.

It hurts. My stomach hurts. I can't stop. I can't look round. I won't go home. I'll go where they can't find me. To the barn, the old Parker barn, Steppin's barn. It was mine before Steppin came. He took it away from me. Now it's his. But it's the only place I can go. I can hide there. I can stay there for ever and ever and never come out.

No one need know. I'll be all on my own and not even Steppin will know. Just hide away from everyone, for ever and ever and ever.

10

In Memoriam

It was my fault. I should have run after Mickey and stopped him. Or run with him wherever he was going. I'd never let him down before. It was the first and only time.

I thought I was doing the right thing, waiting for the Widow. My parents had always taught me not to run away. I suppose I should have stopped Mickey going into her garden in the first place. But I never could stop Mickey. I never wanted to. Being with Mickey was like being in another world, where all the rules of everyday life didn't apply. There was just me, him and the river. And if he wanted to believe that the old woman was a witch, then she was a witch. Or maybe Mickey had bewitched me.

So that afternoon, hearing her shout across the fields, I just stopped. At the back of my twelve-year-old mind I was thinking I could put it right. I could say I was sorry and explain that Mickey wasn't such a bad kid. Maybe if I could placate the Widow, things would get better for Mickey again.

It worked, to a certain extent. I stood there and hung my head and said I was sorry and offered to pay for any damage we had done. She was mollified, at least by me, but swore she was going over to Mickey's place to make sure his father punished him. I begged her not to. I said it had all been my idea. Mickey was in enough trouble as it was, without me dragging him into more.

She harrumphed and said if I paid her five dollars for the damage, she guessed it would be all right. I thought five dollars was about four dollars more than she was due, but I didn't argue. I thought I just had about enough in the box I'd stashed under the bed. I said I'd bring it over the next day and she said if I didn't, both my parents and Mickey's would hear about it. Then she strode off over the fields and I went to look for Mickey.

I found him, in our barn, the rope around his neck, his face all dark and his head at the wrong angle. The body was still swinging. I screamed and screamed and screamed until Mom and Dad came running and found us there.

Dad cut him down and pulled the rope off his neck, but it was obvious that there was nothing that could be done. I was beginning to calm down when Mom said she would go get Mickey's parents.

"NO!" I screamed. "NO! NO! NO!"

Mom and Dad looked at me, wondering what had made even more hysterical. I wasn't sure myself. I just knew that Mickey didn't want to go home. That was why he was here, in our hayloft. This was home for him, as much of a home as he had ever had. It was to our barn, the old Parker barn he called it, that he had always run away to before when he was unhappy at home. It was here he had slept his last night.

"But we have to tell his parents," Mom said.

"I know, I know," I was gasping for breath. "But not yet." Then I realized what I wanted, what Mickey would have wanted. "Take him to the river," I said. "Show him the river."

"But, son," Dad said.

"TAKE HIM TO THE RIVER!" I screamed. I could feel myself going red, my eyes, my lungs, my whole body swelling in anger. I thought I might explode, die like Mickey. "SHOW HIM THE RIVER! SHOW HIM THE RIVER! IT'S HIS! IT'S HIS HOME! TAKE HIM TO THE RIVER!"

My parents looked at each other. There was a confused, scared look in their eyes. I think my mother nodded. Years later I realized she had known about Mickey and me.

The pick-up was just outside. Dad carried Mickey out and laid him on some straw at the back. I jumped up and held Mickey's hand. Mom got in the front. As we bumped over the fields to the river a few hundred yards away, I thought about what Mickey must have done, how he must have felt about me abandoning him. He wouldn't go home. He hated it. I would have too. The more I thought about it as I got older, the more I hated his parents for what they did to him.

In my mind's eye I could see him climbing up to the hayloft. Maybe he waited for me. Together, he would have thought, we could outwit the Widow. We were in love — wasn't that what he had said — so her spells couldn't hurt us. Then when he realized I wasn't following, he would think he had been betrayed by the only friend he had. He had talked about death before. It wouldn't be difficult for him to take the rope we used to haul up the bales, wind it round his neck and jump off.

I told Dad where to stop, so that we could walk the last bit of the way along Mickey's special path down to the riverbank, the path along which we had both walked and run so many times to fish or swim or skip stones or just do nothing. Mickey had been so proud of making the dusty track himself before I came along.

Dad carried Mickey as I walked along beside him, crying my heart out as I held Mickey's hand. Neither my Mom nor Dad said anything, wondering if they were doing right, to obey their son rather than go straight to Mickey's parents.

By the riverside Dad let me kiss Mickey on his blue lips and didn't stop me from running my fingers through his long, beautiful black curly hair, which Mickey had hated so much. I put my head against his silent chest for a moment. It was as if I was listening for him, although I knew inside me that he had gone, he was free of all the ugly things that had happened to him in his life. The sky had darkened and I thought it was sunset. It seemed to me that Mickey was saying goodbye to the sun one last time.

It started to rain. We walked back to the truck, Mickey's exile finally over.

* * *

Sitting by the river — Mickey's river — even after so many years, brought it all straight back to me as if it had been yesterday. There was all the pain of that last day, but also all the wonderful days we had spent together.

Mickey was the one who helped me understand myself. Just by being there, he taught me that I was not the only one who felt like I did. I discovered real friendship — and love — with Mickey.

"Okay?"said a voice behind me.

Mark was standing a yard away. He had followed me down to the river's edge, where I'd sat down watching the river slip by the spot where I had spent that summer. I had asked him to wait in the car for ten minutes, then to come down after me if I did not return.

For a brief moment, I thought... But it was only the light on his face.

The river was stronger and clearer than it had been that long, dry summer when I had first scrambled down to see what the dark-haired boy was doing, the boy I'd first seen the day before when we passed him on our way to our new home.

I remembered Dad telling me it was a tradition in this state for boys to challenge each other to arm-wrestling contests. If the newcomer lost he would have to leave town. Dad liked to joke a lot. It was part of the reason I loved him. He was right about the contest, only it was skipping stones. And we never decided who won.

"Yes, I'm okay," I told Mark. "Just a bit..." I fell silent as he put his hand on my shoulder."I understand," he said gently, knowing how I felt. I had told him all about Mickey when our relationship became serious, as he had told me about the first boy he had loved.

"He was special, wasn't he?"

"He was," I said, looking into Mark's eyes. "I loved him and I..."

I could not continue. I was in floods of tears. Mark dropped to his knees beside me. "Let it out," he said gently, taking me into his arms and stroking my hair the way he always does when we are close. I had taken the band out and let my ponytail down when I got to the water's edge, running my hand through like I used to when I was a kid with Mickey, tucking it around my ear.

I kept on crying, the pain of that summer in my eyes and heart. As I shook with sobs, Mark held me as I had held Mickey all those years before.

"I loved him so much, Mark," I cried. "Why did he do it!? Why? We could have got it sorted out. He didn't have to kill himself! It was so stupid! I loved him! We loved each other."

Mark had no answers, no explanation for why that summer ended the way it did. He just held me and let me cry, venting all the sorrow and anger that I still had inside.

Some of the anger was against Mickey for taking the wrong way out and leaving me alone. Some of it was at myself for leaving him when he most needed me. Most of the anger, however, was at the world, at Mickey's parents, his teachers, his classmates, for everything they had done to him, how they had hurt him.

Mom looked at me with concern when we got back to the farm. She saw my red face and expression. "He's okay," Mark said, as I went to the sink and got myself a glass of water.

I flushed bright red when I saw what my dad had done. He had fixed up my bed and moved the spare bed next to it, roping the legs together and covering the two with sheets and blankets.

"Thanks, Dad... Pop," I said turning to him.

"Well... Steppin," he said, looking me in the eyes as if he was searching for something. "If you... and Mark are... together," he said the word as if it was difficult for him, "then it's only right that..."Mom had known what Mickey meant to me, but Dad hadn't, not even when I'd held Mickey's hand and kissed his lips. He'd gone on for years about pretty girls and made harmless blue jokes. Finally, he'd had to accept it when I told him it was Mark I loved. It was not what he wanted for his son, but I was lucky he took it well. Or maybe it was more than luck. Both Mom and Dad have always been good to me.

"Thanks," I said. "I know it's hard for you..."

"You're our son," he said, looking at me straight in the eye. "As your Mom has always said. No matter what other people say about you, what you want to do with your life has got to be up to you. If you're happy, then we're happy too."

His face darkened for a moment.

"The barn," he said. "I didn't know whether to... but when we knew you were coming, I went over to... to tidy up a bit. In case you wanted..."

"Later on, Dad," I said. "After lunch, maybe."

If you enjoyed this book, you may like the following titles from our extensive fiction list:

Agustin Gomez-Arcos
THE CARNIVOROUS LAMB

The passionate story of two brothers growing up in post-civil war Spain, as soulmates and as lovers.

"A carnal poem, frank, provocative, triumphant"
— *Le Monde*

276pp   0 85449 019 1
UK £5.95   AUS $14.95   (not available in USA/Can)

Tony Duvert
WHEN JONATHAN DIED

This highly acclaimed French novel traces the relation-ship between an insecure artist and a boy of eight.

"One of the most intelligent, bold and subversive books of the year" — *Le Monde*

176pp   0 85449 154 6
UK £7.95   US $12.95   AUS $17.95

Kenneth Martin
AUBADE

A summer romance for Northern Irish teenager Paul that will leave its mark for the rest of his life.

176pp   0 85449 097 3
UK £6.95   US $12.95   AUS $19.95

Recent new fiction from The Gay Men's Press:

S. Joseph Krol
NORTHRIDGE HIGH FOOTBALL CAMP

Big Vinnie Manta — with an ego to match — is new in town. In the high-school football squad, the rivalry between him and Vuch, Northridge's star quarterback, gradually develops into friendship. Football camp turns out to be a riot of beer and hazing, but can Vuch and Vinnie have what you might call a relationship?

224pp   0 85449 225 9
UK £8.95   US $12.95   AUS $19.95

Martin Foreman
THE BUTTERFLY'S WING

Andy and Tom are a well-matched couple in their thirties; Andy works for an international organisation, while Tom looks after their smallholding in Berkshire. Disaster strikes when Andy is kidnapped in Peru by the Shining Path guerrillas, and Tom has to work for his release. Exploring the strengths and tensions of gay love in the 1990s, the story weaves in major issues of the contemporary world scene as it unravels towards a dramatic denouement.

288pp   0 85449 223 2
UK £8.95   US $14.95   AUS $19.95

Gay Men's Press books can be ordered from any bookshop in the UK, North America and Australia, and from specialised bookshops elsewhere.

If you prefer to order by mail, please send cheque or postal order payable to *Book Works* for the full retail price plus £2.00 postage and packing to:

Book Works (Dept. B), PO Box 3821, London N5 1UY
phone/fax: (0171) 609 3427

For payment by Access/Eurocard/Mastercard/American Express/ Visa, please give number, expiry date and signature.

Name and address in block letters please:

Name
_____

Address
_____

_____

_____